PUFFIN BOOKS

the Diary of Dennis THE MENACE

Canine Carnage

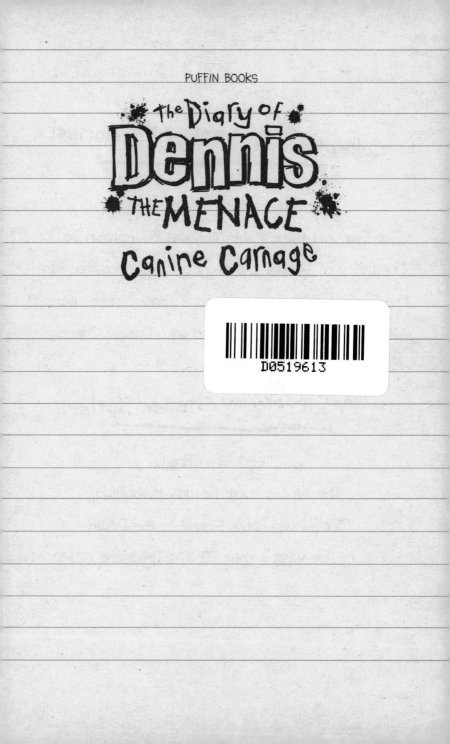

D0519613

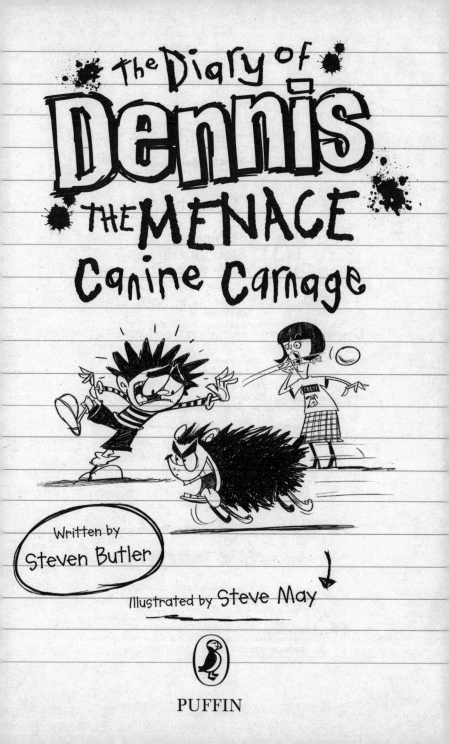

The Diary of Dennis THE MENACE
Canine Carnage

Written by
Steven Butler

Illustrated by Steve May

PUFFIN

PUFFIN BOOKS

UK | USA | Canada | Ireland | Australia
India | New Zealand | South Africa

Puffin Books is part of the Penguin Random House group of companies
whose addresses can be found at global.penguinrandomhouse.com.

puffinbooks.com

Penguin
Random House
UK

First published 2015
This bind-up edition published 2016
001

Written by Steven Butler
Illustrated by Steve May
Copyright © DC Thomson & Co. Ltd, 2015
The Beano ® ©, Dennis the Menace ® © and associated
characters are TM and © DC Thomson & Co. Ltd, 2015
All rights reserved

The moral right of the author, illustrator
and copyright holders has been asserted

Set in Soupbone
Designed by Mandy Norman
Printed in Great Britain by Clays Ltd, St Ives plc

A CIP catalogue record for this book is available from the British Library

ISBN: 978–0–141–37086–6

www.greenpenguin.co.uk

MIX
Paper from
responsible sources
FSC® C018179

Penguin Random House is committed to a
sustainable future for our business, our readers
and our planet. This book is made from Forest
Stewardship Council® certified paper.

For Jeremy Strong –
a clonking great writer,
headmaster extraordinaire and
international menace of mystery

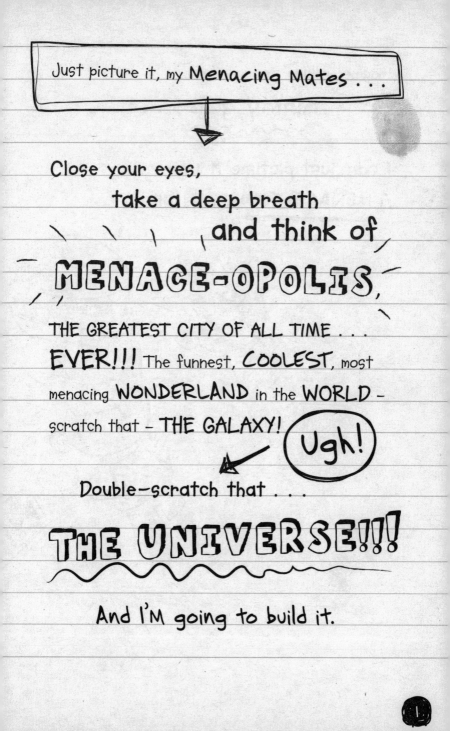

Imagine walking through those

mighty gates . . .

I can just picture it now . . .
A MENACE-TOPIA filled with

video-game arcades, fairground rides, cinemas that ONLY show scary films, sweet shops, junkyards, LOUD MUSIC, circuses and burger bars serving my favourite SLOPPER-GNOSHER-GUT-BUSTIN' BURGERS!

It's going to be BRILLIANT!

Everyone will live in their own super-cool tree houses and right at the top, high above all the other buildings, I'll be the <u>EMPEROR</u> in my very own **TREE PALACE!**

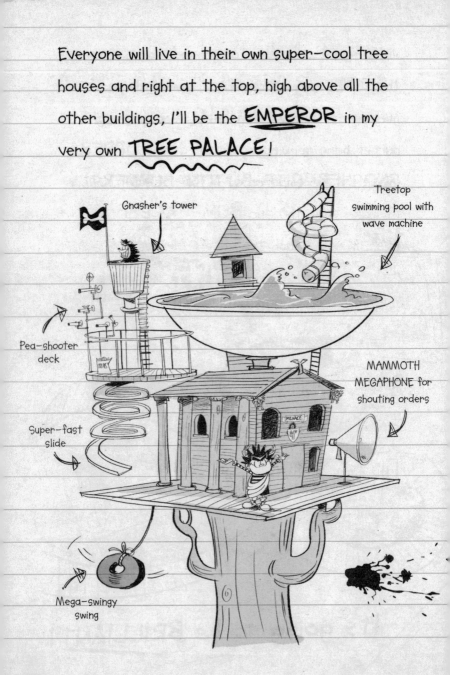

Gnasher's tower

Treetop swimming pool with wave machine

Pea-shooter deck

MAMMOTH MEGAPHONE for shouting orders

Super-fast slide

Mega-swingy swing

And best of all . . .

SOFTIES WILL BE BANNED!

Not one boring, whining, wafty Softy in sight.

When I'm the emperor of MENACE-OPOLIS,
I'll make sure that no **BUM-FACES** can
ever come through the gates. I'll invent special
SOFTY-SCANNER machines that will detect any
BORING-BRIANS or **WHINGEY-WILFREDS**
trying to smarm their way in.

BUT I ONLY
READ WAR AND
PEACE TWICE!

Oh no, wait - I've got a better idea . . .

Instead of banning them, I'll give the likes of
Walter and his bum-faced chums, Dudley and
Bertie, all the rubbish
jobs that nobody else
wants to do . . . like . . .
**THE ROYAL TOILET
SCRUBBERS!** Or the
Royal Fart Wafters
whenever my little sister,
Princess Bea, comes to visit!
OR the **Royal Drain
Un-blockers** after giving
Gnasher his yearly bath! **Ha!**
That would make my
arch-enemy and all
his cronies squirm . . .

It's going to be FANTASTIC!

I bet you can't wait to visit, have a wander

around and . . .

AGH!

WHAT AM I DOING?

CONCENTRATE,

DENNIS!

You don't know **HOW** I'm planning to build Menace-opolis yet! Or about all the money I'm going to win, do you?

I'M SERIOUS, my Menacing Mates.

I'M ABOUT TO BE RICHER THAN RICH!

I'll be able to blow my nose on **£100 notes** when I'm done. <u>Take a look at this</u> . . .

ARE YOU A TOOTIFUL, BEAUTIFUL SINGER?

DOES YOUR GROOVY GRANDMA DANCE A MEAN MAMBO?

CAN YOU JUGGLE FLAMING SWORDS WHILE DOING THE SPLITS IN ROLLER SKATES ON ICE?

WHY NOT COME AND TAKE PART IN BEANOTOWN'S NEWEST TV SHOW,

THE FAME FACTOR!

WITH A GRAND PRIZE OF £1,000!

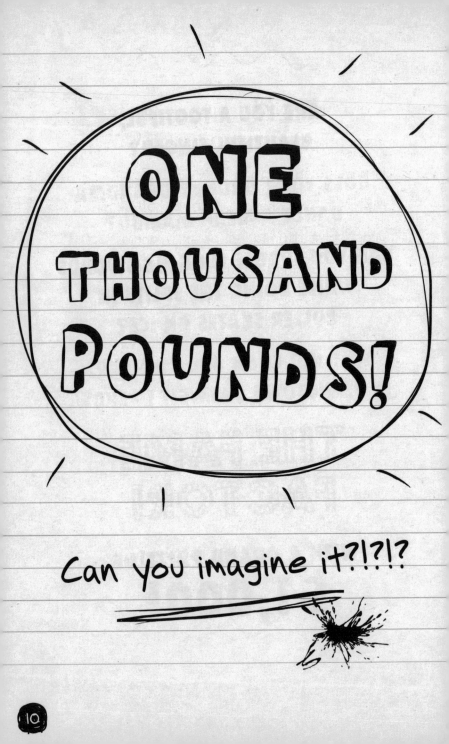

There's **NO WAY** I can lose a talent competition! Who in the **WHOLE WORLD** is more talented than DENNIS THE MENACE? No one . . . that's who! I'm practically stuffed full of skills and tricks. There's nothing I'm not **BRILLIANT** at . . . well, except being a boring **BUM-FACE** - I'M RUBBISH AT THAT! (HA!)

The only thing is, I have to figure out which of my talents is the best. It's just not easy when there are so many of them.

Ummmm . . .

MY LIST OF
MEGA TALENTS

- **Bogey** sculpture

- Whopping-Great-Mega-**Burps**

- Super-Fast-Ice-Cream-Eating

- Conquering Softies

- Shooting Things From Really Far Away With My **Pea-shooter**

- Flower-Bed-**Stomping**

- Squished-Bug-Collecting

- Whiff-tastic **Farting**

- Scary-Face-Pulling

- Marathon-TV-Watching

Hmmmmm . . . I just don't know.

All of those things are AMAZING menacing skills to have, but I need something to really, REALLY **WOW** the judges on The Fame Factor.

It has to be something that will

BLOW
THEIR
BONCES
OFF!

I need to have a really good think about this so I'll definitely be wanting brain food.

Luckily, I noticed a box of Mega—Crunch—Turkey—Tangles in the freezer. They're **MENACE-A-LICIOUS!** Especially if you cover them in ketchup before you scoff 'em down. Mum bought them for me and my best dog-pal, Gnasher, as a treat to say sorry for thinking I was the Bash Street Bandit.

I'll just grab a small portion of **Turkey-Tangles** . . . for medicinal reasons, of course.

(HA!) I can already feel my brain kicking into gear!

What did I tell you, my Trainee Menaces? I knew the Mega-Crunch-Turkey-Tangles would do the trick. Tasty, deep-fried, breadcrumbed, dripping-in-ketchup food always helps me come up with great ideas!

Me and Gnasher were pretty full so we wobbled off to bed to read comic books and let our brain food go down for a while. At first, nothing happened and I couldn't think of my best talent, but then I fell asleep . . .
AND HAD THE CRAZIEST DREAM!

It was genius!

I woke up with ALL the answers racing about in my brain!!! Let me explain . . .

My dream was pretty normal to start off with. Beanotown was under attack from CREECHER-BOT 3000, the giant KILLER robot-teacher from the BOOKY LAGOON, and I was SUPER DENNIS . . . flying through the air in my cape and stripy pants of power, fighting the rancid rust-bucket with my Mega-Zap-Gun and my trusty Laser-powered Pea-shooter.

When I finally defeated the Creecher-Bot, everyone came out of their houses, waving and cheering, throwing chocolate and money at me for being so brave and menacing.

AND THAT'S WHEN IT GOT INTERESTING!

All of a sudden, in my dream, my Mega-Zap-Gun turned into the coolest red-and-black-striped GUITAR! It was **FANTASTIC!** My mates Curly and Pie Face appeared out of nowhere and, before I knew it, we were playing the loudest, **MADDEST**, rockiest concert that Beanotown had ever heard.

I can't believe I didn't think of it before!?!?
It's just the thing to help me win the grand
prize . . . MY BAND!

Me and my Menacing Pals, Curly and Pie Face,
have the best rock band that ever existed.

WE'RE CALLED

DENNIS AND THE DINMAKERS!

The judges at **The Fame Factor** auditions are special guests, and they're bound to LOVE our KILLER rock music and practically throw us through to the **LIVE FINAL ON TELEVISION**. It's going to be so **BRILLIANT!** I can just tell!

£1,000!!!!

With that much money, I'll be able to buy the whole of Beanotown, bulldoze it to the ground and build my own menacing wonderland in its place . . . and put the toilets on top of Walter's garden! **HA!**

There's a whole week until the auditions at the town hall, so me and the boys have plenty of time to rehearse and make sure that we're even ROCKIER than usual. We're going to blow them away with our **AMAZING** tunes.

AGH! I CAN ALMOST TASTE THE PRIZE MONEY!

Fancy-schmancy hat!

Pockets stuffed with money →

More money ↘

EVEN MORE MONEY! →

← Solid-gold shoes!

MEGA-RICH MENACE!

Phew . . . that's better . . .

Anyway, my merry band of Menaces, I'd say it's about time we had a little catch-up. If you haven't had a sneaky peek through my other **TERRIFIC** diaries before, your fun levels must be dangerously low. How have you coped? You've missed out on some serious menacing. I feel so sorry for you . . .

The past year has been **MEGA MENACING!**

(NO!) EVEN MORE MENACING THAN THAT!!! I never imagined I'd be able to fit so many great menaces into such a small amount of time, back when I was first forced to write a diary by my EVIL husk of a teacher-fiend, Mrs Creecher.

She's THE WORST!!!

You will write a diary for an ENTIRE SCHOOL YEAR!

I thought I was doomed when she told me I had to keep a diary as a punishment for not doing my summer holiday homework. I couldn't imagine anything more terrible! I thought I was a goner for sure . . . HOW WRONG COULD I BE?

It turned out to be

MENACE-TASTIC!

What you're holding in your hands
is the fifth of my menacing manuals.

THE FIFTH!

I can't believe I've already filled
four whole notebooks with all the
MENACE-TASTIC things
I've seen and done. I should
get a medal for my menacing
contributions to society,
I really should.

If it wasn't for me, Beanotown would have been taken over by hordes of boring, flower-loving, fun-hating,

BUM-FACED SOFTIES!

Bertie

Walter

Dudley

CAN YOU IMAGINE?

That's not all. There's been loads of amazing and terrifying stuff as well . . . like . . . umm . . . <u>OH</u>! Like mystery Menaces terrorizing the streets, runaway hot tubs, sleepwalking

criminals, **GHOSTS** and **MONSTERS**, LOOP-DE-LOOPY rollercoasters, slobber-choppsy love letters, exploding sandcastles, **demonic librarians**, snowstorms, AMAZING DISGUISES and I even had to eat

VEGETARIAN FOOD!

It's all been a whirlwind, I can tell you . . .

If you've read my other menacing manuals, you're well on your way to becoming a fully trained Menace by now. But never mind if you haven't. You'll catch up soon enough . . . It just so happens that tomorrow me and Gnasher are off for a **TERRIFIC**, menace—filled day at Beanotown Zoo, and it's a great place for you to start your training and learn all about being a tip—top

PRANKMASTER GENERAL.

YIKES! It's past midnight! We've got a busy day ahead of us tomorrow, my Trainee Menaces.

GOODNIGHT!

DON'T LET BORING, BOOKY BUM-FACES BITE!

10.30 a.m.: AND WE'RE OFF, my Menacing Pals. After three quick helpings of breakfast, me and Gnasher bundled up our sleeping-bags and then grabbed as many snacks, comics and bottles of DOUBLE-BURP-BUBBLE-POP as we could stuff into our backpacks. Beanotown Zoo, here we come! You'd love it!! It's one of the most menacing places in town.

I've loved it ever since I was a little Menace and Mum and Dad brought me and baby Bea for the day. There's a **SUPER-COOL** bit when you first come in and you drive your car through the baboon enclosure. **Ha!** I think the baboons liked Dad's car just a little bit too much . . .

Once a year in the summer, the zoo lets customers in for the whole night. **THE WHOLE NIGHT!** It's the most **MENACY** kind of sleepover you can imagine.

SCREECH!

HOWL!

Yep! Beanotown Zoo is a menacing marvel, full of the fiercest, most **fang-gnashing** animals from all around the world!!!

ROAR!

GRRRR!

35

Everyone arrives super early and waits for the gates to open. Then there's always a mad rush to get a spot near the enclosures with the scariest animals.

Well, let's face it . . . who wants to sleep next to the rabbits and gerbils in Princess Pixie's Petting Corner when you can bed down next to the **tigers** or **rattlesnakes**, or snooze in the **vampire bat cave**?

Only Walter and his wimbly-pimbly cronies want to sleep near the **cutesy, fluffy, cuddly** things.

Believe me, I should know . . .

I had a **DISASTER** last year. Ugh!
It makes my spine judder just thinking
about it. I'll tell you, but you'd better brace
yourselves, my Trainee Menaces. It was a

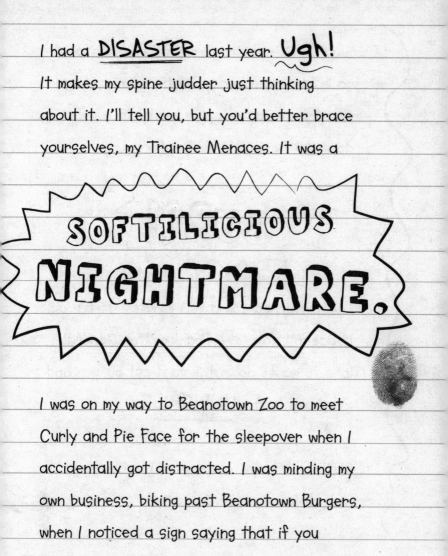

SOFTILICIOUS NIGHTMARE.

I was on my way to Beanotown Zoo to meet
Curly and Pie Face for the sleepover when I
accidentally got distracted. I was minding my
own business, biking past Beanotown Burgers,
when I noticed a sign saying that if you
bought a SLOPPER-GNOSHER-GUT-BUSTIN'
BURGER you got a free chocolate-flavoured

SLURP-'N'-BURP-O-SHAKE! I HAD to go in . . . No Menace worth their stripes would pass up the opportunity to guzzle down tasty drinks that make you

BURP!

I only stopped for a few minutes. After all, it doesn't take the Prankmaster General long to scoff down the tastiest burger and milkshake in the UNIVERSE.

BUT . . . those few minutes cost me very dearly, let me tell you.

When I got to Beanotown Zoo, all the cool places were taken.

IT WAS TERRIBLE!

Minnie the Minx had grabbed the good spot on the bridge over the **Tiger Terrain.**

The **Bash Street Kids** had claimed the **vampire bat** cave.

Curly and Pie Face were in the insect house and hadn't saved room for me in all the excitement.

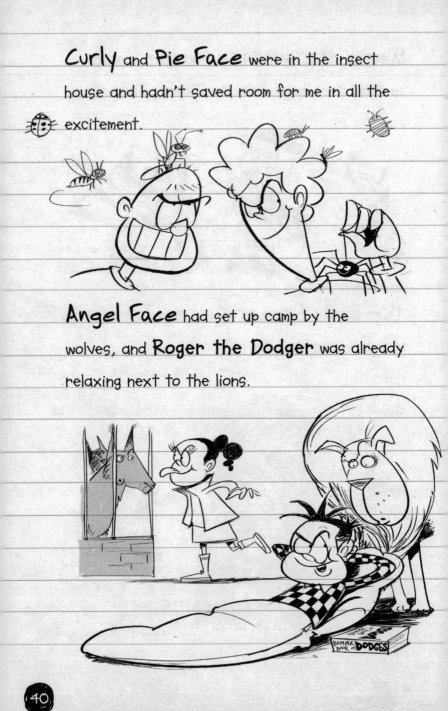

Angel Face had set up camp by the wolves, and Roger the Dodger was already relaxing next to the lions.

Even the **reptile room** had been grabbed by **Bea** and the rest of her pong—tastic playgroup pals.

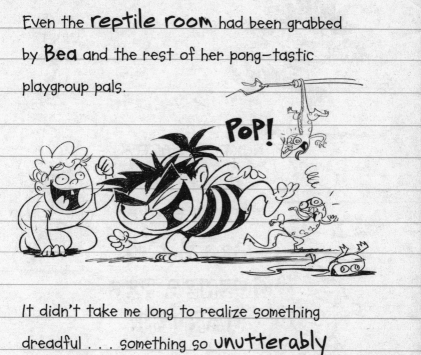

It didn't take me long to realize something dreadful . . . something so **unutterably disgusting** . . . that I nearly **exploded** my shorts right off.

I still find it hard to relive the **memory** . . .

I can barely write it down . . .

The only spot left was . . .

WAS . . .

NEXT TO WALTER,
DUDLEY AND
BERTIE BY THE

GIGGLING
GUINEA PIG
GARDEN!

42

All that boring baby stuff is miles away from the cool, menacing animals on the other side of the zoo.

It was **THE WORST**, my Menacing Mates! I had no other choice but to bed down right beside them! I missed all the best animals and felt like the laughing-stock of Bash Street School for ages afterwards. I couldn't show my face for days. Imagine it! THE INTERNATIONAL MENACE OF MYSTERY forced to pitch his sleeping-bag next to his archest of enemies in the petting zoo ... NEAR THE **GERBILS** AND **BABY GOATS!!!** I've **never** been so humiliated in my life.

To make it even worse, I had to listen to
Walter bawling all night because he thought a
guinea pig had given him an evil glare.

But it's not going to
happen again.

NO
WAY!!!

Today, me and Gnasher are prepared and ready for action. I set my Mega-Bleep-Digi-Clock to wake us up MEGA early and we're off and out, armed with all kinds of menacing tools to help make tonight as fun as possible.

MENACING ZOO ESSENTIALS

- **Marshmallows** for sleepover snacking.

- **Camera** for cool animal photo opportunities.

- **Pea-shooter** in case Walter and his cronies pitch up too close.

- **Lion-repellent spray** (for emergencies).

- **Comics** for a spot of bedtime reading.

- **Double-Burp-Bubble-Pop** for drinky deliciousness.

<u>11.15 a.m.:</u>

WOW!

The zoo doesn't open for another forty-five minutes and there's already loads of people outside the gates . . . I've just seen all the Bash Street Kids, Minnie the Minx and Angel Face jostling to get near the front. Even my menacing gran's here with her pets, Rasher and Gnipper.

Rasher

Gnipper

I'm glad we're prepared this year. Me and Gnasher **LOVE** feeding time the most. All that growling and pouncing and gnawing . . . **BRILLIANT!** That's why we HAVE to get a spot near the best animal enclosures. It's so cool watching the zookeepers feed the bears and lions AND SNAKES. <u>I CAN'T WAIT!</u> Maybe this year they'll see sense and feed Walter to the crocodiles? <u>**Ha!**</u> Actually, I doubt the crocodiles would eat him. He probably tastes like books and <u>**BUM!**</u>

12 noon, lunchtime: We're IN, my Trainee Menaces. Now it's a race to get to the best, BEST, **BESTEST** spot in the whole zoo.

I'M SO EXCITED!

I BET YOU HAVEN'T GUESSED WHAT THE COOLEST SPOT IS, HAVE YOU?

Ok, I'll tell you . . .

THE BEST SPOT
IN THE WHOLE
ZOO

IS . . .
IS . . .

THE GLASS TUNNEL THROUGH THE SHARK TANK!

It's <u>menace</u>-tastic!

If you're first to pitch your sleeping-bag in the aquarium, you get to spend the whole night with **sharks swimming all around you!!!!** It's as if you're at the bottom of the sea!

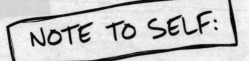

NOTE TO SELF:

ADD A ZOO WITH AN EXTRA-LARGE
SHARK TANK TO THE LIST OF
THINGS I'M GOING TO BUILD IN
MENACE-OPOLIS . . . AND ONLY
I CAN GO IN IT! **BRILLIANT!**

I can't think of a more menacing place to sleep
than the MIDDLE OF A SHARK TANK! We've
got to get there first . . .

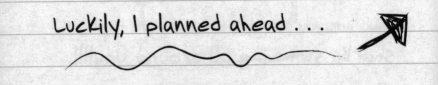

Luckily, I planned ahead . . .

Menacing Lesson no. 359:

There is always a shortcut to be had. No matter what, make sure you know it. Your stripes may depend on it . . .

Me and Gnasher have been visiting the zoo for days to scope out the quickest route to the aquarium. While everyone else darts off in different directions, we can take our time.

It's BRILLIANT!

LOOK!

WHAT DID I TELL YOU, MY MERRY BAND
OF MENACES?

WE MADE IT!!!

Me and Gnasher got to the shark tank in no
time. **HA!** It's going to be an **AMAZING** day,
I can tell. I can't wait to see the faces of
all the other Beanotown Menaces when they
come running into the aquarium and see that
DENNIS and his trusty pooch-pal are still

NUMBER
ONE!

Now that we've pitched our spot in the shark tunnel, we can have fun around the zoo. No one would dare to steal our place with our sleeping-bags there. It's part of the **Menacing Code** . . . and **NO** Softies would ever dare to sleep in the shark tunnel, so there's nothing to worry about from them. Now we can relax, knowing that tonight we're snoozing at the bottom of the ocean. <u>Yes</u>!

AAAAAAANNNDDD . . .

it's not long before feeding time.

I CAN'T
WAIT!

AAAAAAAAAAAGGGGGGGHHHHHH!

Something terrible happened, my Trainee
Menaces . . . It's nearly 8.30 at night
and I should be getting ready to settle
down among the sharks for the most
menacing sleep of my life . . . but where
am I instead?

AT HOME,
THAT'S WHERE!

I just don't understand. It all happened so quickly . . . **it was a blur!** We were just minding our own business and then . . . before I knew it, me and Gnasher were back home . . . in trouble and . . .

And we didn't do anything wrong! Except . . . well . . . **ummm . . .**

I'll explain.

There we were in the glass tunnel, getting ready to watch the sharks eat. I was so excited I didn't notice Gnasher sneak off . . . and then just as feeding time started . . .

The zookeepers in the aquarium threw a bit of a wobbly, but it wasn't Gnasher's fault. It was hours since our three helpings of breakfast and my poor dog-pal must have been hungry . . . really hungry . . . REALLY, REALLY HUNGRY.

Next we went to watch them feed **the lions . . .**

Then there were
the snakes . . .

Noooooo!

It went on and on like that until finally we got kicked out of the zoo by the **BUM-FACED** keepers! Who knew they were **Softies** all along?

Ugh! This is the worst day ever . . . **EVER!** Now I'm going to have to wait a whole year before I get the chance to sleep in the shark tunnel again, and it's all because of . . .

Because of . . .

Agh!

I can't be angry at Gnasher. He's my **bestest pal** in the whole of Beanotown, and who can blame him when there was all that food for the taking? Anyway, Mum and Dad can be angry at him instead of me.

They went bonkers!

Just after we arrived back home, there was a knock at the door. When we answered it, the manager of the zoo was standing there with a face like a smacked bottom. He handed a letter

to Mum and Dad, and kept wagging his
finger and looking angry and babbling on
about this and that and such—'n'—such . . .

YAWN!

I've never seen Mum turn such a bright
shade of purple. It looked like her head
was about to rocket off her shoulders
when she read what had happened.

For Dennis the Menace's Parents,

I am writing to inform you of the dreadful, greedy behaviour of your son's dog, Gnasher. Zoo feeding time was completely disrupted when that mangy mutt decided to help itself to all the animals' lovely mealtime snacks. It was Culinary Carnage!!! I suggest <u>it</u> is taken to OBEDIENCE CLASSES immediately. Next time this happens, you will be paying the food bill for every animal in Beanotown Zoo . . .

Yours sternly,

Albert Tross

Albert Tross
Zoo Manager

'IT'?! WHO IS MR TROSS CALLING 'IT'?

And mangy? No one talks about Gnasher like that. He's **not** mangy! He just needs a bath and has a particular knack for collecting fleas . . . lots of them . . .

Gnasher's the best dog in the **WORLD**. There's nothing he could learn at obedience classes that he hasn't already learned from me, THE PRANKMASTER GENERAL. A dog couldn't wish for a better trainer and a Menace couldn't ask for a better dog.

It's not fair! Grown-ups never understand . . . Don't they realize that I'm about to win the **BIGGEST** talent competition on TV and become a **MEGA-STAR**, and Gnasher is going to be the most famous dog in the world?

Mum and Dad sent us to bed without any **Double Fatties'** double-fat ice cream after dinner.

NONE! Not a dollop! Not a melty drip of the delicious stuff . . . **Such cruelty!**

Ah, never mind . . . I've got a few **Poppin' Jammy Sour-Candy Toaster Tarts** stashed under my bed. Me and Gnasher can snack on those later and forget about this whole sorry mess.

Ha! Gnasher looked so happy with all that exotic zoo food today. It was **BRILLIANT!** He might have ruined our night of sleeping in the shark tunnel, but . . . well . . . I'm proud of him.

Wednesday

10 a.m.: Guess what, my Menacing Mates!?!? I think Mum is up to something.

:Shhh!:

Keep it a secret!

I crept down to breakfast this morning, expecting her and Dad to still be in a proper grump with me, like they usually are after I've been in trouble. At first, I couldn't find either of them, but then I heard Mum on the phone in the living room.

She was talking to the Beanotown Vets and sounded even snappier than usual . . . which is pretty hard to do.

I sneaked up to the door and, by pressing my ear against it and listening carefully, I could hear her nattering away . . . Mum was moaning about Gnasher's bit of naughtiness at the zoo. 'A dog should never run away from its owner like that!'

Check . . . check . . . this is Reporter Dennis coming to you live from outside the living-room door. Mum is in a right strop and she . . .

Agh! She just said, 'I don't care . . . Gnasher deserves it after what he did!'

What are they going to do?

DESERVES WHAT?

BLLLUuuuGGGHHH!

She just said, 'That's the end of it.
Gnasher will never be able to do it
again. NEVER!'

wh...Wh . . . WHAT?

I think . . . I think they're going to
. . . to . . . **AGH!** I can't even say
it! I think Mum and the vet are going
to send Gnasher away . . .

OR WORSE!!!

Dear Mum,

I **heard** what you and the vet are planning and I can't believe you would do such a thing!

All **Gnasher** did was steal a bit of fish . . . and **ham** . . . and **chicken** with **roast potatoes** and those little sausages with bacon wrapped round them . . . and a **banana sundae** . . . and **stinky sardines** from a few **selfish penguins**. I don't think they were even hungry . . .

You will **never** see me and Gnasher again. We're going to **run off** and . . . and

. . . join the circus, live off bugs and twigs in Beanotown Woods, live in a mansion with solid-gold loos and a room just for burping in, after we win a squillion pounds on **The Fame Factor** . . .

AND I WON'T EVEN BUY YOU A CHRISTMAS PRESENT!

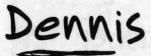

I hope your bum falls off and your arms shrink so you can't scratch it.

Yours sincerely,

Dennis

(formerly known as Your Son Dennis . . .)

OH . . . UMM . . . I think I may have got a
bit carried away there.

Well, what was I supposed to think?

I just heard the next bit of Mum's
conversation . . .

Right!
THAT'S IT!
We're going to
get Gnasher
microchipped!

Gnasher?

Microchipped?

What's that? It sounds . . . It sounds
AMAZING! There's me thinking they were
going to do something HORRIBLE! I don't
know what it means exactly, but imagine how
menacing my best pooch-pal will be after he's
been microchipped. He'll be part MENACING
MACHINE! It's like Mum is rewarding us for
Gnasher's bad behaviour.

MICROCHIPPED!?!?

I can't wait to tell Gnasher. He'll be the coolest dog in history . . . and think how **TERRIFIC** that'll make me, his Menace Master? I'll be able to scare the pants off Walter and every other Softy for miles around with a **robo-dog!**

I don't quite know what all this microchipping is, but I've had a good think and I imagine Gnasher will look something like this when it's all done.

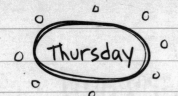

Thursday

1 p.m.: OK . . . so I might have got a bit carried away with that last part as well. Turns out the **microchip** is a bit boring really . . . It was just a weensy thing they put in Gnasher so we know where he is and what he's up to. Poor thing, now he'll never be able to sneak off for a bit of menacing without getting caught. It was so disappointing. I should have known Mum wouldn't do anything fun.

Oh Well . . . never mind. Today I'm meeting Curly and Pie Face in the tree house to come up with something **MEGA-ROCKY** for **The Fame Factor** auditions next week. You hadn't forgotten about that, had you?

We need a **ROCK-TASTIC** new song that's going to blow the judges' socks off and send us straight to the live final on TELEVISION.

Hmmm . . . I wonder what everyone else in Beanotown is planning for their big talent? One thing's for sure . . . none of them will be as **BRILLIANT** as the Dinmakers.

I've already been writing lyrics for our **KILLER** new song.

I'm gonna launch your **gr<u>ann</u>y** into outer space.

She's a **meteor-mama** with a wrinkly face!

WH<u>A</u>M!
BAM!
YOU SMELL LIKE
SPAM!

She's a **<u>BUM-FACED</u>** girl

In a **<u>BUM-FACED</u>** world.

Whatever you do,

Don't let her **breathe** on you!

Mutant <u>**zombies**</u> ate my brain.

Now I slobber and moan

And I'm **TOTALLY INSANE!**

2 p.m.:

We are going to win **The Fame Factor** for sure. Me and the Dinmakers are sounding rock-a-licious and we clearly don't have to worry about anyone else in the competition . . .

It was hilarious!

Me and the boys were in the middle of practice when we heard . . .

> Now come along, chaps. One more time . . . five, six, seven, eight!

There was no mistaking

that voice . . .

From the tree house, you can see most of the houses on my road. We peeked out of the window and, sure enough, there in Walter's front garden was **King Whingerella** himself with Dudley and Bertie. They were wearing the most stupid-looking costumes with long, floppy ears and doing some sort of dance. (Ha!)

The Dance of the Salty Prune Goblin is a wondrous thing!

Such majesty, Walter!

I think I need more bells , . .

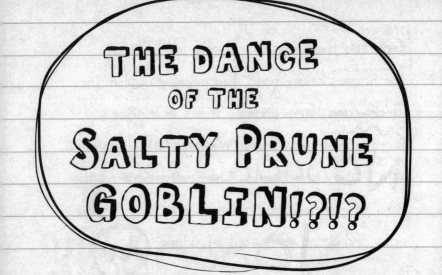

THE DANCE
OF THE
SALTY PRUNE
GOBLIN!?!?

Is that the best old Walter—Wet—Pants can come up with? This is going to be so much easier than I thought. **Ah!** I can just see it now . . . The Dinmakers accepting their **Fame Factor** trophy and **£1,000** prize on LIVE TV!!! I'll be the envy of international Menaces EVERYWHERE!

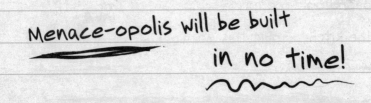

Menace-opolis will be built

in no time!

9.48 a.m.:

NOoooOOooo!!!!

NOooooo!!!

NO-No-No!!

NO!

Just when things were getting better after the Beanotown Zoo calamity, look what Dad left on the kitchen table this morning . . .

Dearest Dog Owner,

Thank you so much for writing to enquire about obedience classes for your Abyssinian wire-haired tripe hound, Gnasher. I'm sure he is a delightful dog and we couldn't be happier to welcome him to the Perfect Pooch Pavilion with open arms and a warm smile.

Gnasher will be an obedient bundle of joy in no time at all.

I look forward to seeing him and his owner for classes over the weekend.

Many thanks,

Olivia Pidd

Olivia Pidd
Dog Trainer

How could Dad sign Gnasher up for obedience classes without telling me? **GNASHER IS OBEDIENT** . . . sort of . . . **Parents can be so sneaky** . . .

I don't have time to skip about in class with Gnasher while he learns how to roll over and beg and let loose **rose-scented farts**. I need to be practising with the boys. We've only got a few days before the auditions.

NOTE TO SELF:

Mum and Dad will be **banned** from Menace-opolis!

The Next Day

I'M SO BORED!

This is torture,
my Menacing Mates.

Dad burst into my room this morning and told me that if I didn't take Gnasher to the Perfect Pooch Pavilion he'd never drive me and my little sister Bea to **Beanotown Burgers** again for as long as we live.

I couldn't do that to my little sister . . . She's such a promising Menace in the making, and a life without **SLOPPER-GNOSHER-GUT-BUSTIN' BURGERS** would stunt her menacing momentum for certain . . .

I HAD <u>NO</u> CHOICE!

11.22 a.m.:

So here I am . . . I can feel Boredom-Brain-Rot setting in for sure. There's no hope, my merry Menaces, I'm a goner this time.

Olivia Pidd, the dog trainer, keeps saying Gnasher will be a bundle of jowly-joy in no time. A bundle of joy? Gnasher is a bundle of something, but it's definitely not **JOY**! Not for the dog trainer anyway! <u>**HA!**</u>

<u>**2 p.m.:**</u> Olivia Pidd has been trying to train me and Gnasher for hours and **NOTHING'S WORKING.**

Now, Dennis, stand up straight, shoulders back and say, 'ROLL OVER!'

ROLL OVER, GNASHER!

5.15 p.m.: We tried playing dead . . .

Maybe he's playing someone who popped their clogs on a roundabout?

I'd never realized how naughty Gnasher was . . .

Ha! That's my boy!

5.37 p.m.: He just gnawed the leg off a table when Olivia told him to 'BEG!'

BEG! I SAID BEG ... BEG!

OBEY!

<u>Haha!</u> When I first arrived at the

Perfect Pooch Pavilion this morning,

I was sure I would have shrivelled

up into a Boredom Mummy by now.

HOW WRONG WAS I?

Watching Gnasher in obedience class was

a **LAUGHTER-FEST!** HE REALLY IS

A BUNDLE OF JOY AFTER ALL . . .

MENACING JOY!

I'm not sure the trainer agreed with me,

but hey, that's what you get for trying

to change a dog that's already perfect

. . . <u>HA!</u>

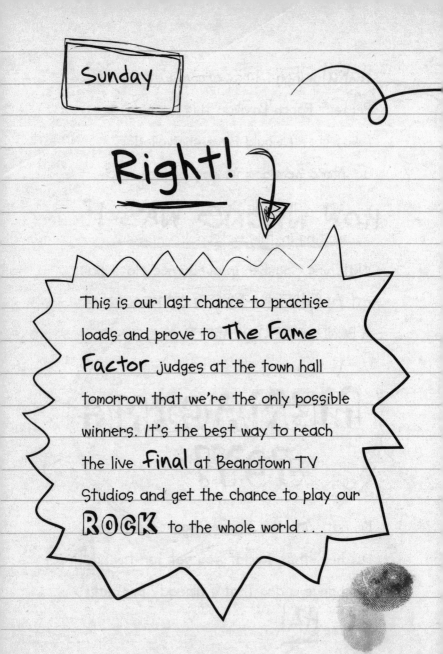

Sunday

Right!

This is our last chance to practise loads and prove to **The Fame Factor** judges at the town hall tomorrow that we're the only possible winners. It's the best way to reach the live **final** at Beanotown TV Studios and get the chance to play our **ROCK** to the whole world . . .

I'd better be off, my **Trainée Menaces**. I've got far too much to do and can't spend the day writing in this notebook.

Don't worry, I'll fill you in on how it goes . . . but you can bet that today's rehearsal will look **something like this . . .**

Monday

__9 a.m.:__

Today's the day, my **Menacing Mates!**

I can't wait to show Beanotown just what the Dinmakers are made of and, thanks to my trusty Mega-Bleep-Digi-Clock, me and the boys are up early and ready to transform ourselves into

KINGS OF ROCK!

It's easy if you know how . . . I just need to get my hands on a few bits and pieces to become an instant _ROCK MENACE!_

10 a.m.:

Me, Curly and Pie Face are about to set off to the town hall. **Ha!** I've just seen Walter waving goodbye to his mum and dad in his goblin get-up. He hasn't got a clue what he's getting himself into . . .

Beating my archest enemy is going to be the most fun **EVER**. Walter always thinks he's better than everyone else . . . I can't believe I'm saying this, but I suppose I can't blame him. At school, he is. Well, Mrs Creecher and Headmaster think he is anyway . . . In term time at Bash Street School, the teachers **LOVE** Walter **SO MUCH** and he comes top of the class in everything. It's no wonder he's such a

Booky-Boring

BUM-FACE!

But we're not at school now and there's not a teacher in sight. The guest judges on **The Fame Factor** are bound to be super cool! I bet they'll run away, screaming

'I'M GOING TO DIE OF BOREDOM-BRAIN-ROT!'

when Walter and his cronies walk on.

BRAIN

That'll show old

WHINGEY-WALTER...

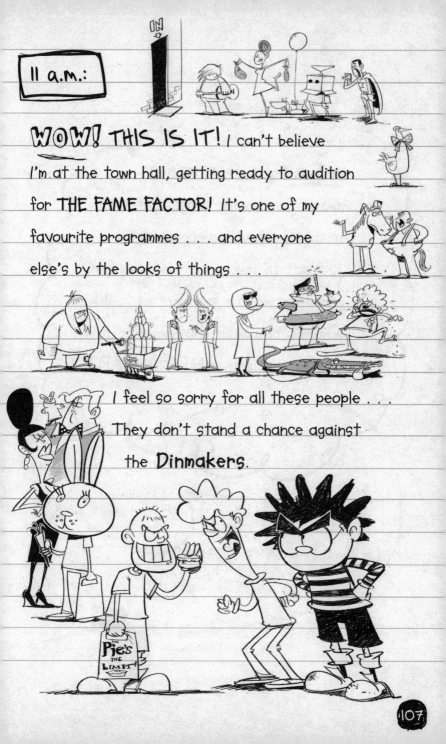

11 a.m.:

WOW! THIS IS IT! I can't believe I'm at the town hall, getting ready to audition for **THE FAME FACTOR!** It's one of my favourite programmes . . . and everyone else's by the looks of things . . .

I feel so sorry for all these people . . . They don't stand a chance against the **Dinmakers**.

11.15 a.m.:

Hmmmm . . . I never imagined there would be so much queuing. We've just got to the end of one long line and been told to join another. Ugh! Where's Bea when you need her to clear a path with a **MEGA-FART**?

I can't wait to get out there and show the judges how amazing we are. They're bound to love our music and put us straight through to the live final.

WATCH THIS SPACE,

My MENACING MATES ...

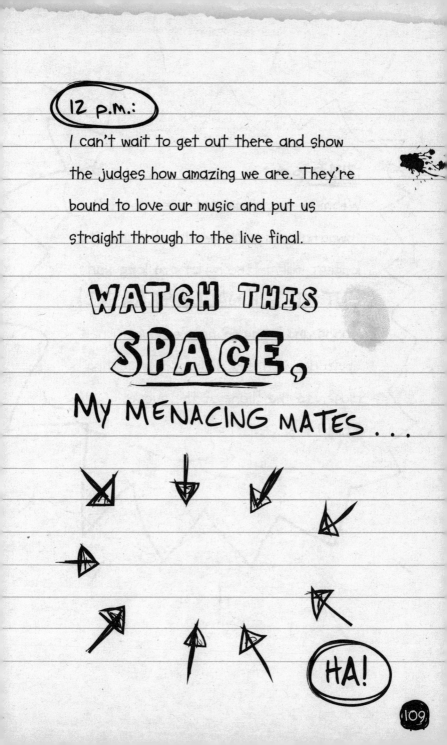

HA!

12.30 p.m.:

We've been standing at the side of the town-hall stage for what seems like the longest wait in the history of long waits, **BUT IT'S FINALLY STARTED!** Loads and loads of people have turned up to audition and we're slowly getting closer to the front of the queue . . . REALLY SLOWLY!

1 p.m.:

Me and the boys are nearly there!

I'm quite nervous.

I'M NOT NERVOUS
AT ALL!

NO!

NEVER!!!

It's been fun watching the other acts from

offstage, though . . .

Minnie the Minx did a roller-skating routine while blowing bubbles with her **Pucker-'N'-Pop** bubblegum . . . That was pretty impressive, but she didn't get through! The judges must be crazy . . . those bubbles were

GINORMOUS!

HA-HAAA!

Gran performed the LOOP OF DEATH on her Charley Davidson motorcycle, with Gnipper and Rasher on the back. I was so proud . . .

BUT SHE DIDN'T GET THROUGH EITHER!?!?!?!

The Bash Street Kids made a human

pyramid, but it didn't go very well . . .

They definitely didn't get through.

Bea shot tin cans off a fake wall from twenty paces away . . . but she didn't get through. Are the judges not watching? That was some of the highest-quality **MEGA-FARTING** I've ever seen!

Then something strange happened.

Mrs Creecher recited her twelve times table while speed-marking homework and giving a wide range of disapproving glares all at once.

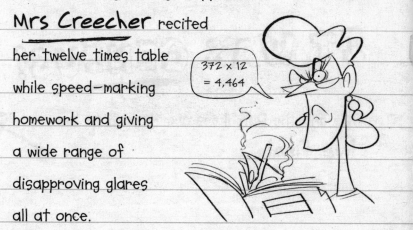

372 x 12 = 4,464

Don't ask me why, but the panel seemed to
love that one . . . I wonder who the mystery
guest judges are? They put her through to
the **live final** on TV!

Mrs Creecher!?

Something weird is going on . . .

3 p.m.:

HA! I never imagined today would turn

into one of my biggest menaces ever.

IT WAS GENIUS!

Me and the Dinmakers are through to the

live final.

YEAH!

Not without a bit of trickery and menacing genius, though.

You won't believe what happened, my Trainee Menaces. **It was a seriously close call.**

Walter, **Dudley** and **Bertie** had just wafted through all twenty-five minutes of the Dance of the Salty Prune Goblin and most of the audience were busy snoring loudly or sneaking off to the snack machines. IT WAS SO <u>**BORING**</u>. But . . . I couldn't believe it . . . the judges **LOVED** it. They actually <u>**LOVED IT!!!**</u>

I could hear them **WHOOPING** and <u>**CHEERING**</u> and they sent the Softies straight through to the live final.

I knew then that something was wrong. <u>**REALLY**</u> <u>**WRONG!**</u> I tried to rack my brains to think what it could be, but . . . that was when they called us up onstage.

There was lots of clapping and cheering from the crowd in the town hall . . . Imagine how pleased they must have been when Walter and his moaning minions were finally gone and a new **MENACE-TASTIC** act was about to entertain them!

I couldn't see very much at first because of all the bright lights. Then I spotted the two usual **Fame Factor** presenters . . .

SIMON SCOWL   GLITZY McTWINKLE

But I couldn't quite get a look at the three
special guest judges . . . The lights were
just too bright.

THEN . . . Just when me and the
Dinmakers were about to leap into
'INTERGALACTIC GRANNY!' and blow
everyone's bonces off, the spotlights dimmed
and I saw the three judges . . .

My jaw nearly hit the floor and rolled away.
Of all the worst people in the **WORLD** to
judge ROCK MUSIC . . .

This next bit is seriously

SHOCKING!

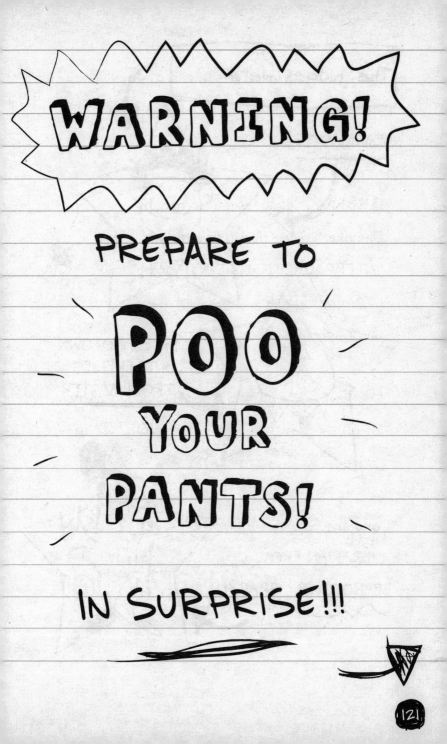

The judges were . . .

HEADMASTER,

the BEANOTOWN
BUTTERFLIES
TROOPMASTER

and the . . .

LIBRARIAN FROM

BEANOTOWN LIBRARY!

122

Those wrinkly old **BUM-FACES** were the secret judges! **WHO** chose **THEM**? It was TERRIBLE! Like a circus of BOREDOM! How can three of the most BUM-FACIEST people to plod across the face of the earth judge an exciting talent show? It was **MADNESS!**

In a flash, I saw everything that was about to happen . . . sort of like a really, **REALLY** boring film in my head. I saw me and the boys playing amazing **ROCK** music. I saw the crowd going wild with excitement . . . AND I saw the three judges shaking their heads and pulling sour faces. Bum-faces like that would NEVER like the Dinmakers. There was no way we'd get through to the final if we played 'INTERGALACTIC GRANNY!' in front of that lot.

Even though it's probably the best song ever
written . . . probably . . .

What were we going to do?

All three of the judges HATED me.
The Troopmaster says I'm a Menace cos
I flattened the new Beanotown Flower Gardens
on my **Rapid Reaper machine.**

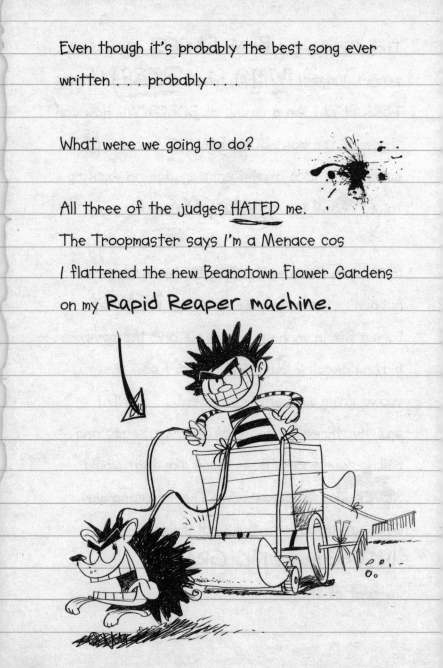

The Librarian has always had her beady eye on me and it's her favourite hobby to **SHHHHH** me if I ever make a sound . . . AND . . .

Headmaster is still grumpier than a bull with bellyache about me locking him in the staff toilets on World B~~ook~~ Menace Day.

I could see them all waiting for me and the Dinmakers to play just one note of music before they threw us on to the rejection pile!

Thinking on my feet, I quickly whispered to Curly and Pie Face and, before Headmaster, the Troopmaster and the Librarian could even think about wrinkling up their noses and sending us off, we played 'TWINKLE, TWINKLE, LITTLE LIBRARIAN' instead.

Ha!

It was one of the first things we learned to play in music class when we started at Bash Street School.

They were gobsmacked!

Headmaster, the Troopmaster and the Librarian were so surprised to like our music they just stared for a moment and then put us through to the final!

Headmaster looked like he'd just swallowed a swarm of bees . . . It was **BRILLIANT** and so worth it!

OK, it wasn't too cool to play 'Twinkle, Twinkle, Little Librarian', **BUT WHAT DO I CARE?** So what if we didn't look like RULERS OF ROCK in the first round? No one bothers about the bit that isn't on TV, and anyway everyone in Beanotown knows that I'm

THE PRANKMASTER GENERAL!

Just wait until the **LIVE FINAL** comes around . . . **ON TELEVISION!** The public get to vote for the winner of that show and, just when they think we're about to play nursery rhymes, we'll hit them with the coolest, CRAZIEST, MOST HEAD–BANGING MUSIC they've ever heard and win the **£1,000** easily.

There's no way anything can go **wrong** now!

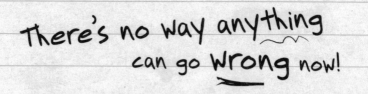

<u>3.25 p.m.:</u>

Forget that last bit!

It looks like we've got trouble, my Menacing Mates.

I had just walked offstage and was heading towards the exit with Curly and Pie Face when I noticed Walter and his cronies sneaking into one of the dressing rooms.

At first, I thought it might be fun to creep up behind them and jump out . . . They always scream like Mum when she's seen a mouse when I do that. It's HILARIOUS!

I was right behind the door when I heard Walter wail. He was SO angry . . .

No! Dennis CHEATED! I heard their rotten song when they were practising!

THEN I heard Walter say . . .

We'll get that HOOLIGAN, chaps. On live television. Just you watch!

- UGH! -

That's just what I need. Walter might be
a WHINGEY-WAFTY-WET-LETTUCE,
but he's a devious little smarmer at the
best of times. I'm going to have to keep
a close eye on my arch-enemy between
now and the live
final. Hmmm . . .

Thursday

I've got **one question** for you,
Trainee Menaces . . .

WHO IS THE GREATEST MENACE
OF THEM ALL?

ME!

I told you I was going to have to keep an
eye on Walter, didn't I? I've followed him
everywhere for the last few days. If I'm
honest, there were moments when I thought
I wouldn't make it . . . I really didn't!

Somehow, Walter manages to fill his days
with only the most, MOST, MOST

boring things a person can do . . . **BUT I GOT HIM!** I know what Walter and his snob—nosed chums are planning to do!

Here's what happened . . . **Super Spy Dennis** in action . . .

I followed him to the art gallery . . .

THAT'S POSSIBLY THE MOST RIVETING JUG AND TOMATO I HAVE EVER SEEN!

THE PHYSICAL IMPOSSIBILITY OF PICKLED SHARK ETC.

On a hike with his scout group, the

Beanotown Butterflies . . .

And even to **Beanotown Burgers** . . .

which was torture!

Everything seemed normal. I didn't spot

a single moment when Walter looked

like he was plotting to ruin the Dinmakers'

performance on **The Fame Factor**.

SO there was only one thing for it, my merry

band of Menaces . . . The oldest tried-and-

tested way of knowing what someone's up to . . .

I had to get my hands on <u>Walter's diary</u>!!!
But he NEVER takes it out of his satchel!

Lucky for us, I know that King Wafty-Trousers goes to synchronized-swimming classes on a Wednesday night. That was the perfect place to pinch it.

Me and Gnasher stood by the big glass window in the entrance hall of Beanotown Swimming Baths — y'know, the bit where you can watch the swimmers if you're too wimpy to take a dip yourself — and waited for Walter to appear.

The minute he skipped out of the changing rooms, ready for his class . . .

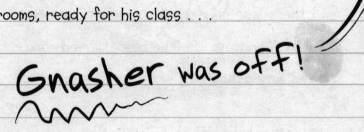

Gnasher was off!

He raced past the receptionist without being seen, into the boys' changing room and made straight for the cubicle where Walter had left all his stuff.

With Gnasher's amazing nose and Walter's unmistakable stink of books and bum, it was pretty easy for my best **pet-pal** to find it.

GNNASH!

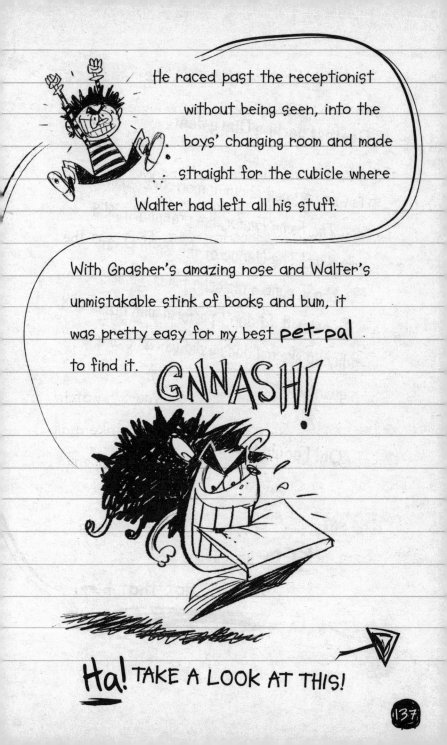

Ha! TAKE A LOOK AT THIS!

Dearest darling Diary dear,

I'm so nervous about tomorrow's audition for *The Fame Factor*, I'm practically all a shudder! The Dance of the Salty Prune Goblin is such a majestic piece. I'll be devastated if I don't perform with grace and dignity like my dadsie did when he was a young chap.

Oh! I could just cry!

Erm . . .
        no . . . not that bit . . .

My dear Diary,

What a day it has been! Naturally, my friends and I were put straight through to the final round on *The Fame Factor*. With gifts of dance like ours, how could we not? I want to feel happy and skip through town with a smile and a song . . . but I don't!

Dennis, that dreadful guttersnipe I've told you about, got through too . . . only his horrid ROCK band didn't play what they were supposed to. Dadsie paid all that money to the boss of *The Fame Factor* to make sure the Troopmaster, the Librarian and Headmaster were the guest judges and it didn't work. I have to do something! I just have to! **Dennis the Menace will NOT triumph this time!**

What did I tell you? It gets even more interesting . . .

I've got it, my Diary-pal!

At tomorrow's live final, after Dudley, Bertie and I wow the audience with our magnificent dance, we are going to ruin Dennis's number. I know what he's planning, the brute. Everyone else may be silly enough to believe that Dennis and the Dinmakers are going to play nursery rhymes, but I'm not.

Before Dennis can let loose a single note, I'm going to turn the volume on the speakers all the way down and yank the button off so no one can turn it up again. Haha! It's brilliant!

Dennis will be humiliated on live television and never come out of his nasty little tree house again!

The End...

I told you **Walter** was a **Smarmer!**

Oh, don't get all worried and start crying this close to the end, my Trainee Menaces. They don't call me the INTERNATIONAL MENACE OF MYSTERY for nothing, you know!

The minute I read what Walter was going to do, I concocted my own plan of attack. I wasn't about to let that Whingey-Wilfred stand between me and building **MENACE-OPOLIS** with my **£1,000** of prize money.

So here's what we're going to do . . .

If Walter wants to turn down the volume on all the speakers in the TV studio, he can . . . because we're not going to be using them.

I borrowed Mum's mobile and called my
MENACE-TASTIC gran. She always
knows what to do when there's a serious
menacing dilemma.

Gran has a supercharged MEGA-loudspeaker
of her own, called the **MEGASONIC
20K** . . . and she says we can borrow it for
the live final.

(HA!)

Walter will bust his bunions when he sees the
Dinmakers have outsmarted him.

Here goes, my Menacing Mates!

7 p.m.:

Agh! I can't believe we're actually here! Inside the Beanotown TV Studios! The place is massive and there are cameras and people running all over with headsets and walkie-talkies.

This is going to be the best night of my life . . . I can just tell. The whole town is in the audience and out there, all around the world, people are settling down in front of their TVs, ready to watch me and my band

ROCK THE UNIVERSE!

The three finalists, Creecher, Walter and his cronies, and me and the Dinmakers are all backstage getting ready to do our stuff.

We've thrown one of Mum's old bed sheets over the **Megasonic 20K** to make sure that Walter doesn't see it until just the right moment. Gnasher is guarding it for now. He's such a good boy . . . Obedience training or no obedience training, he'll always be my bestest pet-pal.

AGH! I can almost see the gates of Menace-opolis rising up before me . . .

IT'S **SO** EXCITING!

7.30 p.m.: WE'RE OFF!!! Simon Scowl and Glitzy McTwinkle have just gone out onstage to start the show. **Phew!** I've got butterflies in my belly . . . Menacing, grizzly-type butterflies, of course . . .

7.35 p.m.: Walter, Dudley and Bertie are up first with their 'trotting troll' dance or whatever it's called. It's a great big snoozefest, that's for sure.

7.45 p.m.: **Ugh!** The Softies are still onstage, prancing about. This dancy thing goes on forever! The poor audience . . . I'll give them about another minute before . . .

Ha!

8 p.m.: Huh . . . Walter finally finished the Dance of the Salty Prune Goblin. I have to hand it to the Softies . . . they're stubborn. Even with the audience booing and shouting, they carried on and finished the whole thing, which means they're still in the competition.

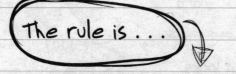

The rule is . . .

IF YOU DON'T FINISH YOUR ACT ONSTAGE, YOU'RE

DISQUALIFIED!

WOW! She's really jazzed up her act. Creecher is still doing her twelve times table and speed-marking homework, but now she's wearing a spangly dress and feathers in her hair . . . and you should see those disapproving looks she's firing in all directions! She looks like a demented gurner on fast forward . . .

Ha!

11,369 x 12 = 136,428!

8.07 p.m.: Wait! Something's happened!

Creecher was in full flow when she . . .

Amazing! Ol' Mother Bum-Face was

disqualified. That leaves just Walter and his

cronies against us. This is too easy! There's

no way we could lose against the Softies.

Haha! I can't help noticing that Walter

seems to be shuffling around very close to the

speaker-volume switches on the wall. I wonder

why that is?

8.10 p.m.:

Here we go, my Menacing Marvels. This is
it . . . the moment we've been waiting for.
This is when I get my **£1,000** prize
and you become fully trained Menaces
just for being along for the ride.

LET'S ROCK!

152

<u>9 p.m.</u>: Sigh . . . What a night!

You should have been here . . .

The last fifty minutes were crazy . . .

We walked on to the stage and pushed the **Megasonic 20K** with the bed sheet over it into place. Then we picked up our instruments and were just about to reveal our big secret when . . .

WALTER LEAPT OUT ON TO THE STAGE, BRANDISHING THE SPEAKER–VOLUME CONTROL BUTTON LIKE A SWORD!!!

I think all this TV stuff had gone to Walter's
head. He turned straight to the camera and
said . . .

This band are a big bunch of
RAPSCALLIONS! They weren't
going to play you nursery
rhymes. They were going to
play noisy ROCK music. BUT I
STOPPED THEM!

I couldn't have asked for a better introduction!
It was AWESOME! I turned to Walter, struck
my power stance and said:

GUESS AGAIN
BUM-FACE!

That's when Gnasher whipped the bed sheet off the **Megasonic 20K** and cranked the volume all the way up . . .

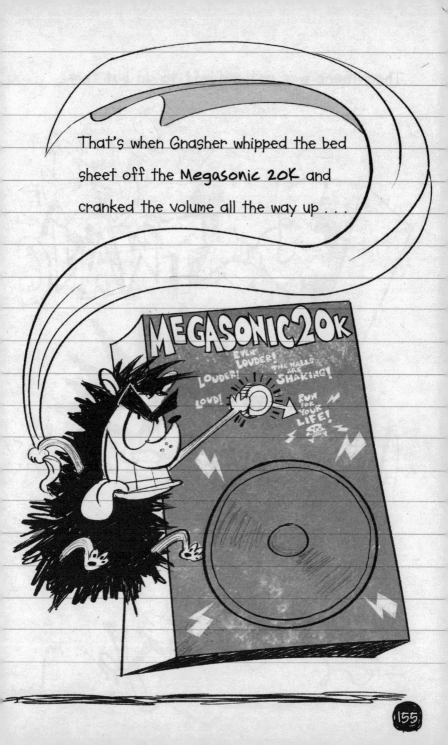

Then there was nothing left to do but this . . .

For a minute, I didn't know what had happened until I managed to untangle myself from Curly and Pie Face. It was AMAZING! I felt like the greatest **ROCK STAR** that ever lived! I couldn't stop laughing until I realized . . .

OH NO!

NOOOOO!!! If we didn't finish our act, we were disqualified just like Creecher, but . . . but the **Megasonic 20K** had exploded into a squillion little pieces and Walter had broken the volume control of the TV studio speakers.

There was no hope . . .

Walter had won . . .

Ha!

You don't think us Menaces would have left old Whingey-Walter with the **£1,000** prize money, do you?

NEVER!!!

The whole place went silent as people slowly clambered back into their seats. Simon Scowl and Glitzy McTwinkle hobbled back onstage and were about to announce the Softies as the winners when something TERRIFIC happened. Gnasher bounded in front of the cameras and started doing all sorts of amazing tricks.

He rolled . . .

He jumped . . .

He walked on
his hind legs . . .

AND THEN HE HOWLED
THE TUNE TO
'INTERGALACTIC GRANNY!'!!!

The audience loved him! All the people watching the TV show from around the world voted for **MY DOG!** It turns out he'd listened to every word that poor old Olivia Pidd had told him at the Perfect Pooch Pavilion . . . He just hadn't been in the mood to obey . . . **HA!**

We went home that night happier than a Menace and his dog could ever be . . .

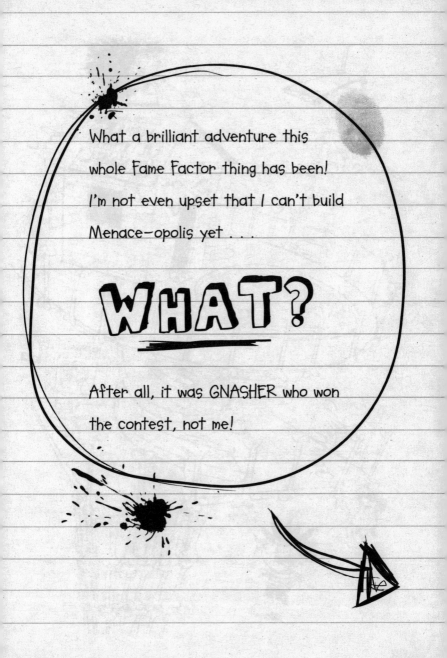

What a brilliant adventure this whole Fame Factor thing has been! I'm not even upset that I can't build Menace-opolis yet . . .

WHAT?

After all, it was GNASHER who won the contest, not me!

THE BEANO®

Where's Dennis?

NEW 'WHERE'S DENNIS?'* APP!
OUT NOW! FREE TO DOWNLOAD!

Over 50 things to find in each scene, plus a two-player head-to-head mode, beat the clock and more.

App Store — Download on the

Google play — ANDROID APP ON

What are you waiting for?
Go download it and get searching!
Ask your parents first, of course, or they'll go bonkers.

Got no tablety thingy?
No worries.
Just get the good ol' fashioned book instead!

Available in all good bookshops (and maybe even some rubbish ones!)

*AND GNASHER!

WHY NOT DO YOUR OWN MENACE JOURNAL?

I've menaced my diary . . . now it's time to menace yours!

Join *The Beano* comic's front-page legend as he guides you through everything you need to know to create a book just like his. Your teacher will hate it!

COLLECT ALL THE BOOKS IN THE DIARY OF DENNIS THE MENACE SERIES!

KIDS RULE IN BEANOTOWN!

WANT MORE DENNIS THE MENACE?
JOIN HIM EVERY WEDNESDAY IN . . .

THE
BEANO ®

www.beano.com

© DC THOMSON & CO. LTD. 2014

QUICK!

As soon as you look at this page, **run and hide!** (But remember to take this book with you!) You're about to read something seriously shocking, my Menacing Mates. Something so **MEGA** it will blow your bonce off! I hope you've got a spare pair of pants handy cos you're going to need them!

QUICKER!!

MOVE IT!!

Hide anywhere . . .

JUST GO!!

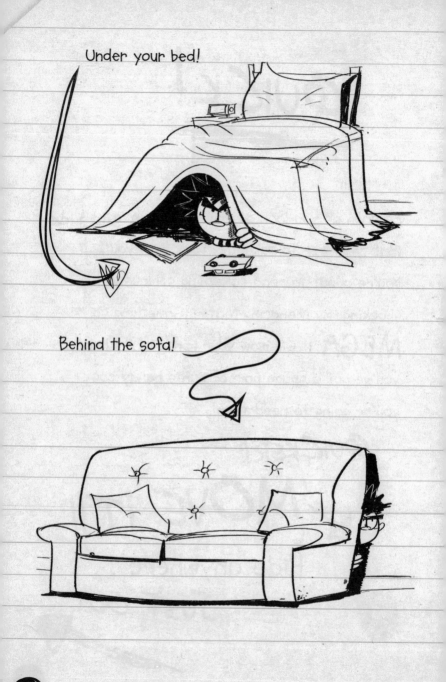

In the cupboard where all
the towels go!

Are you safely hidden?

Good . . .

SOMETHING CRAZY IS HAPPENING!!

Something weirder than the weirdest

weird thing you could ever imagine

EVER is going on in Beanotown!

I don't know how to say this . . . and

you **MUSTN'T TELL ANYONE**
ELSE!

But . . .

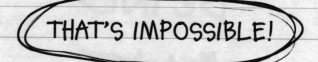

I know what you must be thinking. That the world has gone completely **BONKERS!** How can anyone out-menace **THE PRANKMASTER GENERAL?**

THAT'S IMPOSSIBLE!

I thought that too, but it's true! Just a few nights ago, loads of strange things started happening around Beanotown.

Have a look at this . . . I've been cutting bits out of the *Beanotown Bugle* over the last couple of days. It's a menacing mystery!

BASH STREET BANDIT STRIKES AGAIN!

Reports are coming in of yet another SHOCKING incident!

At 7.30 a.m. Parky Bowles, the keeper of Beanotown Park, was on his morning rounds to water the flowers when he discovered something terrible. During the night, someone had dug up all the beautiful flower beds and replanted the flowers to spell out BUM-FACE!

WHO IS BEHIND THESE DREADFUL CRIMES?

Sergeant Slipper of the Beanotown Police insists that, although the criminal is still at large, they WILL be caught soon.

Replanting all the flower beds to spell BUM-FACE!?!? It's genius! It's **MENACE-TASTIC!** It's just the sort of thing that me and my best dog-pal, Gnasher, would do! The only problem is . . .

WE DIDN'T!

Someone out there is coming up with **TERRIFIC** menacing ideas and doing them before I've even had a chance to think them up. How can it be happening?

I just can't imagine who's doing this . . .

There's more . . .

LOOK!

SHOCKING NEWS!

The Bash Street Bandit is causing havoc around the neighbourhood again. Late last night, as the residents of Beanotown slept peacefully in their beds, the Bandit climbed over the Colonel's fence and meddled with his impressive garden gnome collection.

Each gnome was turned upside down and had its head buried in the lawn. The Colonel woke to find a sea of little gnome bottoms sticking up in the air. A TERRIBLE SIGHT!

It was brilliant! I had the best view from my tree house the next morning. All those bums! The Colonel looked so confused.

But the only person more confused than the Colonel was me. The old grump lives just next door. **NEXT DOOR!** A new Menace was causing mischief right under my nose . . . AND DIDN'T ASK ME AND GNASHER TO JOIN IN!?!?

I've got to find out who's doing these amazing pranks . . . Whoever it is, they're obviously **SUPER** cool and we'll be great mates for sure . . .

The Bash Street Bandit is bound to want to join my band of merry Menaces and we'll cause happy chaos together . . .

There's always room for one more in the Menace Squad!

Maybe the Bandit is shy . . . umm . . . or if they're new in town they might not know that the **KING OF MENACES** lives nearby!

Yep . . . that's it . . . I think!

Oh . . . but what am I doing? I'm getting way ahead of myself. If this is the first time you've clapped eyes on one of my MENACING MANUALS, I should fill you in on everything that's been going on.

Are you sitting comfortably? **HA!**

A whole year ago, my crabby old crone of a
teacher, Mrs Creecher, made me write a diary
as a punishment for not doing my homework.
CAN YOU IMAGINE THE CRUELTY!?!?

DENNIS!

EVIL

Well, my Trainee Menaces, don't throw yourselves
down the loo in despair just yet because it
turned out to be **TERRIFIC!** I had the BEST
year and I got to document every minute of it!
Diaries are actually pretty handy . . .
There were snowstorms and fireworks and
flower—flattening battles with my archest enemy,

WALTER. There were Slopper-Gnosher-Gut-Bustin' Burgers, mega-farts, haunted houses, rollercoasters, amazing disguises AND monsters on Mount Beano!!

When I finally handed in my year-long diary
for Mrs Creecher to read, she went off like a
rocket with a serious case of wrinkles! It was
brilliant! She was so shocked by all the menacing
things I'd been up to that her face turned
purple and she nearly exploded. **HA!**

But that's all done with now . . . It's the
school holidays and I can relax and do what all
Menaces enjoy the most . . .

MENACING
OF COURSE!

It's going to be great. I've got a few days to
investigate and track down the Bash Street
Bandit, have fun with my pals, Curly and
Pie Face . . .

Something MEGA is happening! Mum and Dad are taking me and my little sister Bea on holiday . . . HOLIDAY!! It's been ages since we've had one. The only thing is, Mum and Dad won't tell us where we're going. Mum says it's going to be the best surprise EVER!

AGH! I can't wait . . .

But that's not for another few days, which gives me and Gnasher plenty of time to find the Bash Street Bandit. If they *are* new to Beanotown, I should give them the chance to find out all about me, **THE PRANKMASTER GENERAL**.

Tonight, after Mum and Dad have finished watching *The Great Beanotown Bake Off* on telly and have gone to bed, I'm going to sneak out and stick posters in the coolest, most menacy places around town. The Bandit is sure to see them.

IT CAN'T FAIL! Here's what I'm leaving in all the cool spots . . .

Dear Bash Street Bandit,

You lucky thing! I bet you didn't know that you're menacing in the stomping ground of the GREATEST MENACE THAT EVER LIVED!

Come and join Dennis's Menace Squad.

Meet tomorrow, 12 noon at the TOP-SECRET tree house in Dennis's back garden.

NO BUM-FACES ALLOWED.

From **Dennis**

Oh . . . bring snacks!

Tuesday

11.55 a.m.: I can't wait to see who the Bandit is . . . Me, Gnasher, Curly and Pie Face are all here in the tree house waiting for the new prankster to arrive. **ONLY FIVE MINUTES TO GO!** Curly even grabbed us a massive bottle of Triple-Dribble-Bubble-Pop from his mum's fridge. It's the best drink in the WHOLE WORLD and the perfect welcome treat. The Bandit is in for a SUPER BRILLIANT afternoon. **HA!**

12.25 p.m.: OK, so the Bandit's a bit late, but will be here soon . . . any minute now . . . any minute . . .

12.30 p.m.: Hmmm . . . still no Bandit.

19

12.42 p.m.: Errmmm . . . well . . . maybe they're just running behind . . . y'know . . . Maybe they had an important menace to do before coming like . . . umm . . . like farting through a Softy's letterbox! That's mega important! Or . . . um . . . GAH! Where is the Bandit?

1 p.m.: Nope . . .

2 p.m.: STILL NO BANDIT . . . and Gnasher has drunk all the Triple–Dribble– Bubble–Pop. It serves the Bandit right for being so late.

3 p.m.: OH BUM!

BUM!

BUM!
BUM!
BUM!

D'you know . . . I don't think the Bash Street
Bandit is coming. There's no way they could
have missed the posters. I stuck them up
everywhere. They were in all the best, most
menacy spots around Beanotown.

Maybe the Bandit just doesn't want to join
my squad.

I . . .

I . . .

AGH! GET A GRIP, DENNIS!
WHAT AM I WORRYING ABOUT?

No one, not even a grown-up, would be

stupid enough **NOT** to join my MENACE

SQUAD. Maybe the Bandit is just too

nervous to come forward.

I AM MEGA-IMPRESSIVE
AFTER ALL!

I'll just have to find the Bash

Street Bandit myself. It won't take

me long to figure out who it is.

I AM THE . . .

INTERNATIONAL MENACE
OF MYSTERY!

With my secret-agent skills, I'll find the Bandit before too long. Especially now that it's the school holidays . . . I have loads of extra time to investigate without boring old Bash Street School getting in the way of my detective work . . .

OPERATION UNMASK THE MYSTERY MENACE!

Hmmmm . . . Think, Dennis! So there's a Menace in town who's ~~just~~ as nearly as menacy as me . . .

SO WHO IS NEARLY AS MENACY AS ME?

Not even my pals Curly and Pie Face come close!

CURLY

PIE FACE

Before all this started happening, I'd have thought nobody was as MENACING as me . . .

IT'S CRAZY!

Finding the Bandit is going to be tricky. It could be anyone . . . well . . . almost anyone.

One thing's for sure: it's easy to eliminate the people who absolutely CAN'T be the Bash Street Bandit.

Let's see . . .

First of all there's my WET-PANTED arch-enemy, Walter. Look at him . . . The bum-face of all BUM-FACES! He's as smarmy and devious as they come, but he can't be the Bash Street Bandit . . . There's just no way!

NO-NOOO-NOPE!

It can't be Sergeant Slipper. He's head of the Beanotown Police Department and is always trying to solve crimes, not commit them!

WAY TOO WELL BEHAVED!

Not cunning enough. Loves stopping Menaces!

There's **NO WAY** it's Mrs Creecher or Headmaster!!!! BOOKY-BORING BUM-FACES!

Too dull. Hates anything fun. Too stupid to think up menacing plans.

And it can't be the Colonel . . . Why would the old husk meddle with his own precious gnome collection? He loves those things more than anything in the world.

Poppycock!
It's not me!

Well, that's the 'NO' list sorted . . . The only problem is, there are LOADS of other less boring people that COULD be the Bash Street Bandit.

I'm going to have to keep a lookout for evidence, my Trainee Menaces. If the Bandit is nearly as menacing as me, it's going to be tricky . . . **BUT!!** Even the greatest of menacing masterminds leaves the occasional clue. If I keep my eyes peeled, I'm bound to spot something.

Hmmm . . . I think it's probably a good idea to have a spot of brain food before bed. Just to make sure my powers of clue-spotting are in tip-top condition, should anything happen during the night.

I'll just make myself a teensy Double Fatties' double-fat-butter-banana-chocco-scotch sundae to take to bed with me . . .

WHAT!?!

I'm going to share it with Gnasher and . . .
y'know . . . it's just for medicinal, thinky
purposes.

I can already feel
myself becoming a
better detective!

Me and Gnasher are going to start our
investigations tomorrow.

I CAN'T WAIT . . .

Wednesday

9 a.m.: Hold on to your stripes, my Menacing Mates. We're off **ALREADY!** The Bandit doesn't waste any time . . . the twisty troublemaker has been at it again.

When I came down for breakfast, Dad was fussing and grumbling over the newspaper as usual. Looks like the Bandit can't keep away from menacing. The prankster really is like me!!

I JUST HAVE TO KNOW
WHO IT IS . . .

33

Read this!

THE BANDIT IS BACK!

The curators of the Beanotown Museum were baffled this morning when they discovered that the Bash Street Bandit had broken into the building late at night and caused Cretaceous chaos with the exhibits.

Who is behind these terrible acts of mischief? Sergeant Slipper and the Beanotown Police are baffled.

9.30 a.m.: **Right!** Here's the plan . . .

Later, me and Gnasher are going to check the

BUM—FACE flower beds in Beanotown Park.

There's bound to be something old Sergeant

Slipper and his policemen haven't noticed.
They're not the brainiest bunch.

But first we'd better head off to the museum
and search for clues before everything gets put
back in order.

Ha! I never thought I'd go to the Beanotown
Museum without being dragged there, kicking
and screaming, on some awful school trip.
But with my Menace's brain and my **MEGA-
MENACING** detective kit we're bound to
spot something.

Oh, I just thought! You probably don't have a
MEGA-MENACING detective kit yet. Well,
don't panic! It's easy to get your hands on all
the things you'll need.

THE
PERFECT
MEGA-MENACING
DETECTIVE KIT

- **A magnifying glass**

  for super-snoopy spying.

- **My Insta-Pic-Camera** that

  Gran bought me a few Christmases

  ago. It's great for snapping speedy

  pictures of suspicious clues.

  (And taking photos of your bum

  and sending them to your enemies!)

○ Mum's Flaky-Feet talcum powder for fingerprint dusting.

○ A snack for if you get hungry (VERY IMPORTANT).

○ A hat with funny ear flaps. All good detectives MUST have a proper ear-flappy hat. I pinched mine from Dad. He likes to wear it when he goes fishing with his workmates . . .

YAWN!

11.27 a.m.: <u>HA!</u> I've just arrived at the museum and it's the best, most menace—tastic thing I've ever clapped eyes on. You should see it, my Menacing Mates. The museum was closed because of the incident and covered in Beanotown police tape . . .

The museum guides were so flustered and confused, they barely paid any attention to me and Gnasher. I just shouted, **'I'M A DETECTIVE! OUT OF MY WAY!'** and walked right in. <u>HA</u>!

Now I'm inside, I can't believe my eyes!

It's a menacing marvel!

No, scratch that . . .

IT'S A
MENACING
MASTERPIECE!

The Bash Street Bandit is clearly a genius. **A PROPER, PROPER ONE!** Already I can really, REALLY tell that we're going to make a great team . . . when I finally figure out who it is.

The museum's ANCIENT BITS AND BOBS room has been completely menaced from top to bottom!

Better get detecting . . .

11.45 a.m.: GOT SOMETHING!! Searching for clues was a seriously tricky business, my Trainee Menaces. The Bash Street Bandit had left such a mess that it was hard to tell what was what.

We searched all over the **ANCIENT BITS AND BOBS** room and couldn't find a thing. I was about to give up when . . . GNASHER SNIFFED OUT OUR FIRST CLUE!

He started barking and growling at the T-rex's skull on the floor. At first I thought Gnasher was just making a fuss because he loves to chew bones and this one was a whopper, but then I noticed something caught in the monster's massive teeth. It was a piece of the special school notepaper used for letters to our mums

and dads . . . The kind with the Bash Street
School emblem on it. It must have got stuck
there when the Bandit was pulling off the
Tyrannosaurus's head.

Ha!
I'M ON TO YOU, BANDIT!
FOILED BY A
DENNISAURUS!!

I should have known the T-rex would come in
handy with our investigation, though. Dinosaurs
are **FANTASTIC** . . . even when they're
dead!! You can bet that all dinosaurs were
MEGA-MENACING back in the old-olden-
OLDY days.

I wish I had a pet dinosaur. I could train it to eat Softies and then poo on teachers. It's such a shame they're not around any more. I bet Menaces and dinosaurs were great pals back in the Dino-days . . .

What am I saying? It looks like we still are! HA!

12 noon:

CHECK . . .

CHECK . . .

OVER . . .

This is Detective Dennis and his trusty hound, solving crimes and getting one step closer to finding the Bash Street Bandit.

Our first clue is a scrap of school notepaper. So one thing's for sure . . . the Bandit must go to Bash Street School.

Hmmm . . .

KEEP MENACING!

We may be one step closer, Menacing Mates, but we're not close enough. Loads of people go to Bash Street School. On the last day of term, Mrs Creecher gave us a ton of **BORING** letters about this, that and such–'n'–such to take home for our mums and dads to read.

Anyone with half a brain would have squished them up into little balls with their spit and fired them at the back of Creecher's head with their pea–shooter, but there's probably loads still lying around in the bottom of people's school bags.

The Bandit must have had a school letter stuffed in a pocket or backpack or something. That means it could be anyone. **UGH!** EVEN WALTER!?!? **Ha!** What am I saying? Of course it's not Walter.

ONWARDS, MY MENACE SQUAD!

We'll have to look for more clues down at Beanotown Park. I'd better get over there and have a poke around.

We'll figure out who the Bandit is before you can say BUM-FACE!!!

3 p.m.: What did I tell you, my Trainee Menaces? When I got to Beanotown Park, there was a big crowd of people, all chatting and gawping at the **BUM-FACE** flower beds.

(HA!) IT WAS HILARIOUS!

It looked like half the town was there to get a look at the Bandit's handiwork. Even Walter! Yep! Lord Softy McSoftison was right at the front of the crowd, wailing and gnashing his teeth about how terrible it was that the roses and pansies had been tampered with. **HA!**

Normally I'd steer clear of Walter and his

booky, <u>BUM-FACED</u> cronies, Bertie and Dudley,

but I noticed they were talking to Parky Bowles,

the park keeper. I crept as close as I could

and hid myself behind one of the bins near the

flower beds to have a good listen.

AHA! So the Bandit broke into Parky Bowles's gardening shed to find the tools to dig up all the flowers. I think I'd better start looking in there.

This is Detective Dennis on the trail. I'll let you know what I find . . .

3.25 p.m.: *I DID IT!* I found our second clue and it's a SUPER juicy one. My detective skills are better than ever. Thank goodness for the Double Fatties' double-fat-butter-banana-chocco-scotch sundae I had last night. It's clearly the best brain food a Menace can eat!

ANYWAY, I managed to sneak into Parky's shed when he wasn't looking and have a good rummage around. There was just a load of rusty old shovels and rakes and hoes and not much else, except spiderwebs and mouse poo. It all seemed pretty hopeless when suddenly I spotted . . . there . . . on the wall . . .

THE BANDIT HAD LEFT A WHITE, CHALKY HANDPRINT!

Thanks to my MEGA Insta-Pic-Camera, I got a good photograph of it for evidence . . .

CLUE
NUMBER 2

Chalky
handprint

KEEP MENACING!

The Bash Street Bandit was using chalk right before breaking into Parky Bowles's gardening shed. It also explains the chalk writing on the wall at the museum. That's got to narrow it down, surely?

THINK, DENNIS!!

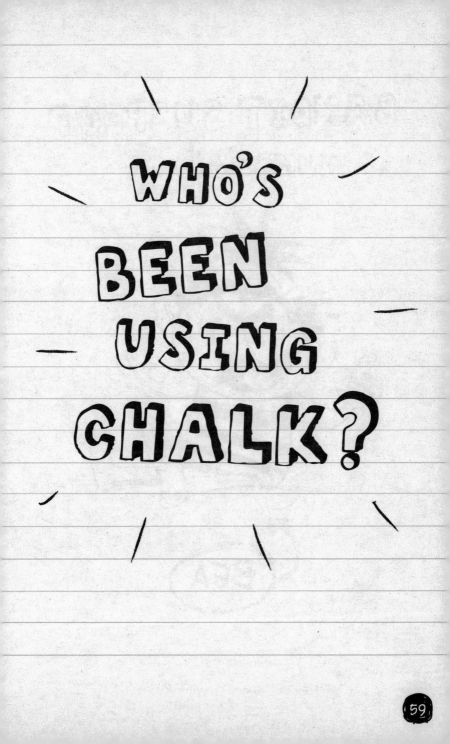

I know my little sister Bea loves to play with her chalks at home. She's always drawing all over her bedroom walls with them and making Mum go bananas.

It couldn't be my little sister, could it? She's certainly a mini-Menace AND she's learned from the best. But Bea doesn't go to Bash Street School yet and wouldn't be tall enough to climb up and reach the T-rex skull in the museum!

BANDIT SUSPECT
NUMBER 2

MINNIE THE MINX

Just two days ago, I saw Minnie
drawing Hop-the-Bog-Frog
games on the pavement outside
Mr Har Har's Joke Shop.

Minnie is a **SUPER** menacy **MINX**.
She could definitely be the Bash
Street Bandit!

This is growing more and more
MYSTERIOUS by the minute.

The Bandit goes to Bash Street School
and was using chalk right before they
replanted the Beanotown Park flower
beds. **Hmmm . . .**

There's only one thing for it, my Menace Detective Squad. If me and Gnasher are going to rack our brains and figure out who the Bash Street Bandit really is, we're going to need EVEN more sweet, sugary brain food. HA!

I'm off home to have a think and eat myself smarter. Catch you later . . .

Midnight:

STOP

EVERYTHING!!!

I . . .

   I . . .

      I can't believe it . . . .

It's too shocking . . . My brain might explode.

Something . . . Something . . .

OH, SPIT IT OUT, DENNIS!

Something MEGA happened earlier tonight. It's

all a bit of a blur . . . I . . . I would have blown

my bonce off with surprise if I wasn't so brave.

After all this . . . the Bandit is . . . is . . . is a

BUM-FACED ENEMY!

Let me explain . . . It was ten o'clock and I was sitting on my bed with Gnasher, eating my way through a third helping of minty-creamy-crumble-crunch ice cream when we heard the most enormous scream.

AAAAH!

It was massive and squeaky and irritating and I knew straight away who it belonged to. The only person that can shriek that high in all of Beanotown is . . . **WALTER!**

By the time I darted downstairs and ran out into the front garden, half the street was awake and coming outside to see what all the hoo-ha was about.

Walter was in front of his house, wearing his teddy-bear onesie and being a right Whingey-Wet-Pants! He was wailing like you've never heard anyone wail before . . . like a demented **Softy rooster!**

I ran over to get a better look and saw that he was kneeling over something furry on the ground. As all the neighbours started gathering round, Walter picked the furry thing up and we realized that it was his pampered pussycat, Claudius.

At first I had no idea what was going on.
Walter just kept screaming and crying. But
then he turned Claudius round and . . .

I couldn't help but laugh. **BUM-FACE** is one of the funniest **words** in the world, second only to **BOTTOM-BURP, KNICKERS** and **PIDDLE-PANTS!!** How could I not laugh?

It really was genius . . . Changing the flower beds in Beanotown Park to say **BUM-FACE** was one thing, but shaving it into the fur of **WALTER'S CAT** was something else. It was **BRILLIANT!**

But . . . I bet you're wondering what I was talking about before. How can the Bandit be a bum-faced enemy when they'd just pulled off the best prank Beanotown has ever seen on the most irritating

WHINGEY-WILFRED EVER?

Well, hold on to your knickers and I'll tell you . . .

It was just then that everything went wrong!! **EVERYTHING!!** Walter, that little smarmer, turned on me quicker than Gnasher on a fresh can of Gristly-Giblet-Jumble dog food!

Like I said, I couldn't help laughing at Walter and his *purrrr*-fect cat . . . It was SO funny! The only problem was, Wet-Lettuce-Walter didn't find it quite as hilarious as I did. Before I knew it, he spun round, pointed at me and started shouting . . .

Walter just blew his bonce off! He was
sweating and pointing and wouldn't stop
shouting, 'YOU'RE ALWAYS MENACING ME,
DENNIS! YOU DID THIS! YOU DID THIS!'
Well, you can guess what happened next . . .

Every stupid grown-up in the crowd started staring at me and looking angry. Why do grown-ups believe everything they're told? Anyone with half a brain would ~~NEVER~~ listen to a Whinge-Bottom like Walter! But they all did . . . Even Mum and Dad were glaring at me and shaking their heads!

In no time at all, Sergeant Slipper showed up and started asking questions.

It was AWFUL, my Menacing Mates . . .

I thought I was RUINED!

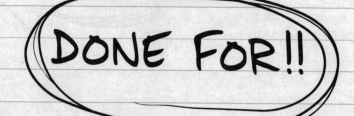

DONE FOR!!

I didn't even have time to run like the wind before Sergeant Slipper put me in handcuffs . . . HANDCUFFS! For a nanosecond, I saw my whole life flash before my eyes.

That part was BRILLIANT, but then I saw what the future of the human race would be like if it was deprived of my MENACY BRILLIANCE! Imagine a world without me, **THE INTERNATIONAL MASTER OF MENACING**, in it? There would be no one to train up future Menaces. No one to hold off the hordes of skipping, sappy, smarmy SOFTIES. It was like watching a **TERRIFYING**, flower-filled horror movie.

Imagine it . . . Years in the future and Lord Softitron has taken over the world and turned everyone into flower-loving bum-faces!

In the Menace—less future, there are bum—faces everywhere you turn. People even have bum—faced babies!

It was just too horrible!

Slipper was about to cart me off to Beanotown Police Station. I would have been thrown in jail for certain if it hadn't been for what happened next . . .

DUN-DUN- DAAAH!

Just as I was about to abandon all hope of ever menacing again, there came another bigger wail, **EVEN LOUDER** than Walter's screaming. It was **SO** loud that everyone spun round.

It was coming from my tree house, over the other side of the road, and I knew that **IT WAS GNASHER.**

Now Gnasher has loads of types of howls
and I recognize and understand all of them.
This one was a very particular howl indeed.
Let me explain . . .

Menacing Lesson no. 9987:
A good Menace always understands his dog.

Your dog can get you out of even
the worst scrapes if you know what
to listen for. Pay special attention to
what it's saying.

DENNIS'S DOG-HOWL DICTIONARY!

First there's the **HOOOOOOOOO!** kind of howl. That means 'I want a Slopper–Gnosher–Gut–Bustin' Burger **NOW** or I'll probably die of hunger . . . or **BITE** you!' Obviously . . .

Then there's the **RRAAAOOORR!** kind of howl. That means 'BEA'S FARTED! DIVE FOR COVER!'

The **RUUUUUUUGH!** kind of howl means 'Walkies . . . PLEASE!?!?'

And the **GROOOOOOOR!** kind of howl means 'Teachers! RUN FOR IT!'

BUT . . .

There's one kind of howl that's saved for only the **WORST OF MENACING EMERGENCIES.** It's the

WOWoWOWoWo!

kind and that's the exact same howl that Gnasher was using.

My heart froze . . . I knew something **TERRIBLE** must have happened. Something more terrible than the most terrible, **TERRIBLE** thing that ever happened in the world. Scratch that . . .

THE UNIVERSE!

It was just then that I remembered that

SOFTY SERGEANT SLIPPER was a

crinkly old grown-up. He couldn't stop me . . .

I'm DENNIS THE MENACE! Before he

could even think about grabbing me, I wriggled

out of his adult-sized handcuffs and darted

between his legs.

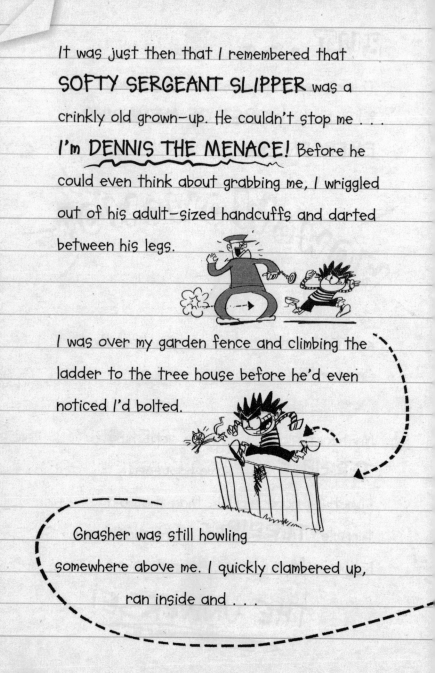

I was over my garden fence and climbing the

ladder to the tree house before he'd even

noticed I'd bolted.

Gnasher was still howling

somewhere above me. I quickly clambered up,

ran inside and . . .

WARNING!

What you are about to read will make your head blow off with shock!!!

My Menacing Mates, it was a **TERRIBLE** sight. At first I thought I must have gone stark raving batty. How could it be true?

While we were all across the road, looking at Walter wailing at his fat cat's new haircut, **THE BANDIT MENACED THE TREE HOUSE!!!**

THE MASTER OF MENACING WAS MENACED! How could this have happened? It was chaos . . .

The Bandit even unravelled my spare Menace's sweater!

I had to give Gnasher three extra helpings of ice cream after all that. My poor **GNASH—TASTIC** pal was pretty shaken. Unfortunately, he had his head buried in a box of Poppin' Jammy Sour-Candy Toaster Tarts when the Bandit struck so he didn't get a good look or sniff at the tree—house trasher.

I've never heard of anything like it. Who would be crazy enough to menace the best pet—pals of the King of the Softies **AND THE PRANKMASTER GENERAL** on the same night?

The plot has just got a whole lot thicker, my Trainee Menaces. Thicker than the gloppy gravy in the Bash Street School canteen. **And that's REALLY thick!**

Hmmm . . .

I'm going to have a quick think. Let's look at the evidence . . .

It just makes no sense . . . Who would be the enemy to Softies AND Menaces? The stripy tie that Gnasher was tied up with is a

SUPER
BIG
CLUE!

But everyone from Bash Street School has got one of those . . . even the teachers! So who could it be?!

BANDIT SUSPECT
NUMBER 3

ANGEL
FACE

Angel Face is Headmaster's daughter and is only

interested in her own mischief. She'd definitely

menace me and Walter on the same night. I bet

Headmaster has loads of stripy ties too . . .

It would be easy for Angel Face to pinch one.

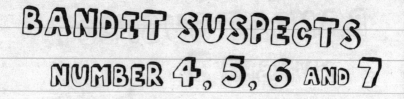

BANDIT SUSPECTS
NUMBER 4, 5, 6 AND 7

Spotty, 'Erbert, Smiffy and Fatty from Bash Street all wear stripy ties. Hmmmm . . . but everyone knows they do. They'd be practically handing themselves in . . . The Bash Street kids would never menace a Menace, would they?

The Bash Street Bandit must be INSANE! BONKERS! LOOP-DE-LOOPY-LOOP!! Who would menace Softies and Menaces at the same time?

What . . . what if . . . what if the Bandit has come to steal my menacing crown?

What if they've come to overthrow me and rule Beanotown forever? I'll be humiliated. No Menace would ever take me seriously AGAIN!

~ NO SOFTY would ever take me

seriously again either.

THIS IS BAD, my Menacing Mates.

Sergeant Slipper let me off the hook after he

saw that I'd been menaced too, but only for

now. I know that old GRUMP still thinks I'm

guilty . . . and Walter does too. If I'm going

to stop the Bandit before I get thrown in

Beanotown Jail, I'll have to work quickly . . .

Really quickly!

THE BANDIT BALLOON

Giant balloon filled with Bea's mega-farts.

I wait for the Bandit to sniff out the bait and cut the rope from behind the bush.

Slopper-Gnosher-Gut-Bustin' Burger . . . No true Menace can resist them.

BYE-BYE, BANDIT!

Thursday

8.30 a.m.:

AAAAAAAAAAAGGGGGGHHHHH!

In all the Bandit-finding excitement,
I completely forgot we're going on HOLIDAY
today. Mum just shouted up the stairs and told
me to bring my suitcase down to the front door.

SUITCASE?

I haven't even STARTED packing my menacing
holiday essentials . . . and **WHAT ABOUT
THE BANDIT?**

If I'm out of Beanotown, the Bash Street Bandit will be free to cause chaos wherever they choose. What if my tree house is wrecked again? What if they take over my **TOP-SECRET** fort in the junkyard?

I don't even have time to build the Bandit Balloon I invented.

UGH! It's horrible, but there's no use worrying about it, I suppose. The Bandit will still be here when I get back and will probably have left a load of new clues by then . . . COME ON! CHEER UP, DENNIS, YOU'RE GOING ON HOLIDAY!

I'm going to have the best time of my life . . . I just know it!

Mum and Dad still won't tell me and
Bea where we're going, which means
it must be somewhere

SUPER,

SUPER

AWESOME!!

Time to get packed or Mum will
throw a wobbly. I'd better not leave
anything to chance.

Let's think . . .

HOLIDAY ESSENTIALS

- Shark-repellent spray.

- Yeti-spotting guidebook.

- Masks and snorkels for deep-sea menacing.

- Catapult with EXTRA mud-ball ammo, in case of local Softies.

- Safari camouflage sweater.

- Inflatable crocodile for pool-time fun.

- Ropes for mountain climbing.

- Inflatable dinghy for white-water rafting.

- Flameproof pants, in case of volcanoes.

- Extra-Sour-Candy Toaster Tarts for desert island survival.

- Lion-bite antiseptic cream.

8.45 a.m.: Right, that's all done . . . **Agh!**
I can't wait! It wasn't easy getting all my
holiday essentials into one case, but I managed
it with a little help from Gnasher.

9.30 a.m.:

BLAST OFF!

Dad bundled our things on to the roof of the car and we were away. I can't wait to see where they're taking us.

I've never seen my parents look so excited. They still won't tell us where we're going, but Mum's practically eating her own head with happiness. This is going to be **TERRIFIC!**

Since I have the best detective skills in the world and probably the biggest brain as well . . . probably . . . I've narrowed our holiday destination down to a few final choices. It just has to be one of them . . .

Yep, it's definitely one of those holiday destinations . . . I'd bet my stripes on it!

I'll let you know when we arrive, my Trainee Menaces . . .

IT'S SO EXCITING!!!!!

9.37 a.m.: That's weird. Dad has just driven the car over the bridge by the river. The only thing over that bridge is Mount Beano and the woods . . . Oh well . . . We must be driving straight over the top of it and onwards to our TREMENDOUS holiday destination.

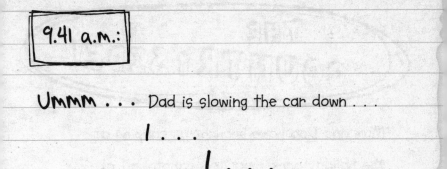

Ummm . . . Dad is slowing the car down . . .

I . . .

I . . .

NOOOOOOOOOOOO!!!

Is this some cruel joke? Are Mum and Dad playing a trick or have they gone round the bend? It's too awful . . . It's too terrible . . . It's **TOO BORING!**

I have two words for you, my Menacing Mates. The most dreadful words there have ever been in the history of really, really, **REALLY** boring words.

THE COUNTRYSIDE!

Mum and Dad have brought us camping at
the holiday park next to Beanotown Lake.
That's it. No tropical jungle islands . . .
No adventures at the bottom of the sea . . .

How am I going to use my SHARK-REPELLENT
SPRAY when we're camping in Beanotown Woods?

Mum says I should be grateful because the
countryside is a beautiful thing . . .

BEAUTIFUL? BRAIN-NUMBING, more

like! There aren't any cool animals around here.
Where are the KILLER SPIDERS or GIANT
ANGRY RHINOS? Nothing exciting EVER happens
in the countryside.

You'd be lucky to get **ants in your sandwiches** and **squirrel poo in your sleeping bag!** This is going to be the worst holiday of my life. I'm stuck at Beanotown Campsite in the middle of the woods while the Bash Street Bandit is probably riffling through my top-secret stuff and stealing my menacing crown.

MY LIFE IS OVER!

I'll probably be dragged off by skipping, singing chipmunks in my sleep, or I'll get Boredom-Brain-Rot and they'll find me in fifty years' time living in a cave on Mount Beano, wearing nothing but a leaf and the longest beard in history.

10 a.m.: Already bored . . . Suddenly those skipping chipmunks seem like a treat!

10.27 a.m.:

Can barely keep my eyes open . . .

So . . .

Much . . .

Green . . .

10.56 a.m.: Does anyone know how to attract ferocious Menace-eating badgers?

11 a.m.: Given up hope of having my head bitten off by Menace-eating badgers . . . Mum and Dad have been fiddling around with the tent for over an hour now. That'll serve 'em right! **Ha!** Dad looks like a furious tomato (his face is so red!) and Mum is all tangled up in the support ropes.

I suppose this is slightly making up for the disappointment of camping. **HA!**

4 p.m.: After six hours of pulling, groaning, sweating, grumbling, heaving and saying rude words that mums and dads aren't supposed to say, the tent is up.

Dad says we're going to build a campfire next, which isn't so bad, I suppose . . . but then he announces that we're going to forage for forest greens and cook baked beans over the fire in one of Mum's rusty old camping pans. Forest greens and baked beans . . . With my **TRUMP-TASTIC** little sister??? If the tent doesn't inflate and float away in the night, it'll be a miracle! And baked beans are vegetables too . . . **AGH!!!**

---

6 p.m.: **Hmmm . . .** I may not be completely sunk after all. While Mum, Dad and Bea tucked into their baked beans, me and Gnasher sneaked off and found the campsite shop over at the far end, by the lake.

<u>GUESS WHAT?!?!</u> They sell Greasy—Battered—Turkey—Twists like the ones from Bash Street School canteen. Turkey—Twists are one of the few edible things that Olive the dinner lady serves up at lunchtime.

I can easily survive on Greasy—Battered—Turkey—Twists while we're out in all this . . . this nature . . . and they have no vegetables in them whatsoever! **DELICIOUS!** Luckily, I brought my week's pocket money with me. That should just about cover my Turkey—Twist rations for the next few days.

This is survival at its most

EXTREME!

9 p.m.: OK, so I may have overreacted just a teensy bit about camping and skipping chipmunks. Tonight was actually SUPER FUN.

Mum and Dad took me and Bea to the observatory up on the top of Mount Beano. At first I thought it was going to be mega boring and a proper snoozefest, but it turned out to be brilliant!

The telescope on the front of the observatory is **HUGE** and you can see all the stars and planets like they're right in front of you.

I bet no one has ever taught you about all the different menacing constellations in the sky, have they? Of course they haven't! There isn't a teacher in the world who is cool or brainy enough to know about them. Well, listen carefully, my Trainee Menaces. I'll give you a quick crash course.

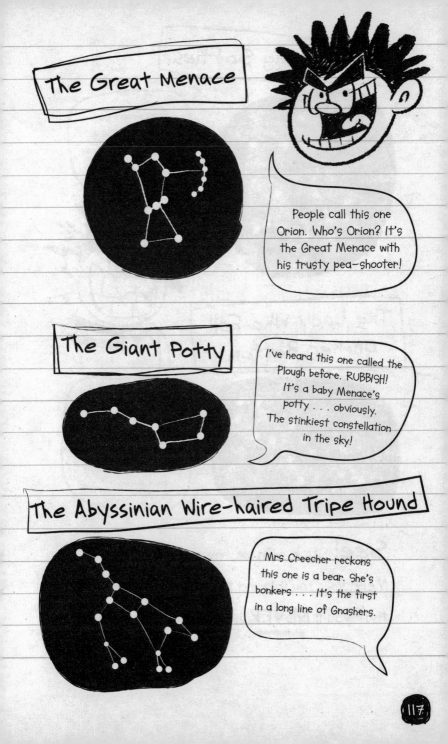

The Skipping Softies

Some people call this one the Twins. Twins? Look again!

The Lady Who Fell On Her Bottom

This one is sometimes known as Virgo. Dad says it's named after an ancient Roman snooker player, but he's wrong . . .

See! Stick with me, my merry band of Menaces. You'll learn things from my diaries that you'll **NEVER** hear in school.

10 p.m.: Mum's making us all go to bed **EARLY** . . . but it's not too bad. Dad's promised to take us out on a boat on the lake tomorrow so the sooner we're asleep, the sooner we can do some more fun things.

There are stories of the great Beanotown Lake monster that lives down in the deepest parts of the lake.

People have been coming here for years from all over the world to try and get a photograph of it. I bet lake monsters would LOVE Menaces.

If the monster's out there, it's bound to show itself for me . . . With my trusty Insta-Pic-Camera, I'll probably get a great shot and become a squillionaire.

Maybe camping is pretty

MENACE-TASTIC

after all . . .

GOODNIGHT!

Friday

8 a.m.: UGH! Something . . . something's happening . . . I just woke up and the ground is shaking. At first I thought it was just Dad's snoring, but it's not. It's something

— BIG! —

I'm going to investigate, my Trainee Menaces.

I'll report back as soon as I've seen what's causing it . . .

8.30 a.m.:

I . . .

I . . .

can't . . .

believe . . .

I CAN'T
BELIEVE
THIS . . .

I must be cursed or something. Surely no one
in the world is having worse luck than me at
the moment?

FORGET the Bash Street Bandit!!

FORGET nature and bird-watching
and flipsy, fluttery butterflies!!

I've just seen the most devastating sight

OF MY LIFE!

I crawled out of the tent to find out what was
making the ground shake and came face to face
with the most enormous camper van I've ever
laid eyes on. It was massive!

IT WAS BIGGER
THAN A BUS . . .

It drove right up and parked next to our
tent . . . and then . . . and then the door
flew open . . . and . . .

Walter's family have plonked themselves next
door to our tent. It's bad enough living so near
that **BUM-FACE** in Beanotown! I can't
bear having him right by me on holiday as well.

IT'S RUINED!!

AND . . . to make it even worse . . . Walter's holiday home on wheels is unbelievable. Just after they parked, Walter's dad came out and clicked a little remote control with a red button on it and the whole thing sort of . . . UNFOLDED! It's . . . it's . . . IT'S NOT FAIR! Why is **THE PRANKMASTER GENERAL** stuck in a tiny tent with his snoring mum and dad and farting little sister when Walter's family arrive in total style? You should have seen it!

I can barely bring myself to say this, but
Walter's holiday home is the coolest thing
I have **EVER** seen.

That Smarmy–Smarmer was up on the top deck
birdwatching with a huge grin on his face . . .
Until he saw me. **HA!**

Then he got all scared and started crying for
his mumsie! He was wailing, 'It's that hooligan,
Dennis! The Bash Street Bandit has followed us
here!'

Can you believe it?!

UGH! He's such a BUM–FACE!

Walter knows I can't be the Bandit. How could
I be when we were both menaced on the same
night? He's just sticking to his story because

he knows he can get me in trouble. Sergeant Slipper believes anything that Walter and his posho mum and dad say. They're **SO ANNOYING!**

Menacing Lesson no. 9999:
Softies will do their best to ruin your fun at every opportunity. Make sure you stay one step ahead and ruin theirs first!

After Walter kept on shouting, his dad put down his barbecue tongs, grabbed a rolled-up newspaper and started shooing at me like I was some stray cat.

SHOOING ME!?!?! It'll take more

than a Softy waving a newspaper to make

THE KING OF THE MENACES run away.

Oh well, now that they're here, I might as well have some fun. It's not like Walter doesn't deserve it . . . Just this year alone he's tried to scare me with a fake Halloween party at Number 13 Frightville Avenue, filled Beanotown with flowers to attract hordes of skipping Softies and tried to trick me out of being the first person in the world to ride the Vomit Comet at Beanoland theme park. He's a devious little whinger.

Hmmm . . . I think it's time I repay Walter for pointing the finger at me in front of Sergeant Slipper.

2 p.m.: So we're out on Beanotown Lake in one of the little wooden boats that Dad hired from the campsite shop.

It's brilliant! Just after the
newspaper–waving incident, I heard Walter's family talking about going out on the lake as well for a spot of fishing. I got straight to work and slipped a note under their holiday–home door . . .

I made a copy just in case.

LOOK!

Dear Bum Faces Holidaymakers,

Just a letter to warn you that if you go out on Beanotown Lake you run the risk of being eaten by the lake monster. Sightings are becoming more and more frequent, and it especially loves the taste of El Snobbo Caviar and bow ties.
You have been warned.

Beanotown Campsite Manager

I knew Walter would fall for it. He's such a fraidy squirrel!

Just before Mum and Dad went to hire our boat, I saw Walter and his parents marching off to get theirs. Walter was crying and moaning, 'No, Dadsie, I don't want to get eaten . . . PLEASE!'

It was HILARIOUS!

What happened next was a stroke of

MENACING GENIUS!

(Even if I do say so myself.)

Once we'd rowed round the lake a few times, Mum and Dad got tired of pulling the oars and decided to take a little nap. That's when me and Bea struck. I love my little sister. She's turning out to be a right menacing marvel.

We waited until Walter and his family were happily fishing and then we made use of the inflatable crocodile I packed for pool playtime . . . and it's a good thing I brought those masks and snorkels after all.

CAUGHT SOMETHING!

Ha! You should have seen Prince Smarmsalot's face when he reeled in the deflated crocodile . . . AGH!

That's when Bea let rip with her greatest talent . . .

HA! I've never seen anyone row to shore so fast . . . That'll teach Walter for being such a **BUM—FACE** and his dad for waving a newspaper at me. Like that's going to frighten me . . .

UGH! THE NEWSPAPER!

In all this **HOLIDAY HILARITY**, I've completely forgotten about the Bandit. I need to get back to Walter's camper van and get a look at that paper. Maybe the Bash Street Bandit has struck again . . .

I won't be long, my merry band of Menaces. I'll keep you posted . . .

8.30 p.m.: Ugh! Thank goodness Walter's family are all Softies and go to bed super early. I could see the newspaper on the table by the barbecue, but Walter's mum and dad sat next to it the whole evening. The minute they toddled off, I grabbed it. Walter didn't come outside once. Ha! I heard his mum saying that he'd locked himself in the bathroom and wouldn't show his face!!!

Anyway . . . have a LOOK at this!

THE BASH STREET BANDIT HAS STRUCK AGAIN AND CAUSED UTTER CHAOS AT THE BEANOTOWN LIBRARY!

During the night, the Bandit broke in and switched the dust jackets of every single book in the building.

One startled victim had this to say:

'I checked *Knitting For Beginners* out of the library, but when I got it home and opened it, it was *How to BELCH in Spanish* . . . I was SO startled!'

Who is committing these terrible crimes?

It's so strange . . . Every time the Bandit has struck, it's always been in a place of interest to <u>B</u>ORING, <u>B</u>OOKY <u>B</u>UM-FACES.

There was . . .

- The **flower beds** in Beanotown Park
- The Colonel's gnome collection
- **Beanotown Museum**
- Walter's house
- **My tree house** (every BUM-FACED Softy would love to get a look in there)
- And now Beanotown Library

What am I missing, my Trainee Menaces?

I wish I was back in Beanotown right now. I can't solve anything from up here on Mount Beano. **Hmmm** . . . if only I could get hold of Walter's binoculars. That way I might have a chance of spying down into . . .

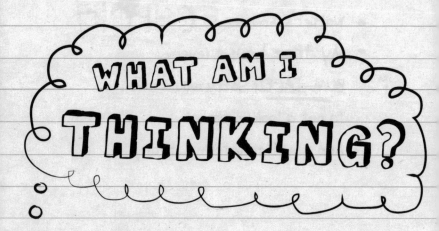

I don't need Walter's rubbish little binoculars! I've got the best piece of spying equipment in all of Beanotown right under my nose . . .

THE OBSERVATORY!

Quick!

10.17 p.m.:

CHECK . . .

CHECK . . .

OVER . . .

CHECK!

This is Secret Agent Dennis

reporting live from the Mount Beano observatory.

Getting in was a piece of cake thanks to my bestest pooch-pal. When we arrived, the doors were all padlocked shut, but Gnasher bit through them like they were made of jelly.

Here goes . . . I think I can figure out how to work this telescope thing. Let's try something easy to start with . . .

Ha! There's my room. **BRILLIANT!**

~~~~~

So we know the Bash Street Bandit only strikes in places that Softies are interested in . . . Um . . . how about . . . Headmaster's house?

Ugh! YUCK! Headmaster is so weird,
but that's normal! All headmasters are weird.
Nothing out of the ordinary there . . .

Ummm, how about the town hall? Softies love
it there . . .

Nothing strange going on there . . .

I KNOW!!!

School is irresistible to Softies . . . they love it! CAN'T GET ENOUGH!

Nothing on the climbing frame . . .

Everything looks normal in the school canteen . . .

How about . . . ?

GUH! THE BANDIT IS
   MENACING OUR CLASSROOM!!!

HA! Mrs Creecher is going to be so angry . . .

I HAVE TO CATCH THE BANDIT! I'VE
GOT TO GET BACK TO TOWN . . .

                    AND PRONTO!!!

147

Midnight:

WOW!
W-O-W!!

What a night . . . That was one of the craziest things that has ever happened to me, my Menacing Mates. You won't believe it when I tell you . . .

After spotting the Bandit in our classroom, I raced back to the campsite to get Bea and Gnasher. If I was going to catch the Bandit once and for all, I needed my **MENACE SQUAD** with me.

First things first, we had to find some wheels. There was no way we'd make it in time if we ran . . . **We needed some serious speed.** I grabbed Bea's pushchair out of the back of Dad's car, but it was no use. Oh . . . it had wheels, but it wasn't nearly big enough for me, Bea and Gnasher to get in together.

That's when I had a **MEGA** idea. We needed something big enough to fit all of us and fast enough to get us into town before the Bandit finished menacing Bash Street School.

THE CATCH-THE-BANDIT-MOBILE

Bea's turbo-powered wind for acceleration

Pop!

Walter's family hot tub

The wheels from Bea's pushchair

Attaching the wheels to Walter's hot tub was **SUPER** easy. I got a few of Dad's tools from the car and I can be mega quiet when I work because I'm an **INTERNATIONAL MENACE OF MYSTERY.** The big problems started when I pulled the plug to drain the water out and it sloshed all over the deck and washed the barbecue over the edge with a massive

Before I could do anything, Walter ran out on to the pool deck and caught us red-handed.

Walter looked like he'd seen a ghost . . .

A GHOST TRYING TO STEAL HIS HOT TUB!

He went **BANANAS** and ran towards us, flailing his hands around like a daddy-long-legs . . . and then . . . then Walter did something I wasn't expecting. He jumped into the tub!

He was wailing and yelling, 'I'VE CAUGHT YOU, DENNIS! YOU ARE THE BASH STREET BANDIT!'

Well, I wasn't about to let Whingey-Wet-Pants stop me when we were so close to nabbing the Bandit. Walter would soon see that it wasn't me if he came with us, so I turned to Bea and shouted, **'NOW!'**

IT WAS AMAZING! There's no turbo power in the world like a gassy little sister.

We went tearing downhill towards the town and Bash Street School! It was faster than the Vomit Comet rollercoaster!!

Gnasher sat at the front and sounded the alarm to alert the whole of Beanotown. If we were going to catch the Bandit, I wanted everyone there to see it.

POP!
POP!
POP!

We'd nearly reached the school gates
when I suddenly realized we had no
brakes. I forgot to build any on the

Catch-the-Bandit-Mobile!!! The only way to stop was to crash straight into the school gates . . . IT WAS MEGA!

When we'd finally untangled ourselves
and clambered out of Walter's runaway
hot tub, I saw loads of the other kids
from school coming out of their houses
in their pyjamas. I can always count on
Gnasher to raise the alarm.

I ran ahead to the front doors of
the school and saw that someone had
picked the lock with what looked like a
brooch pin.

What kind of kid
     wears a brooch?

I peeked inside and everything was dark and silent. There's something **SUPER** creepy about being in school when it's dark, so I was mega pleased when I saw Minnie, the Bash Street Kids and Angel Face arrive at the gates behind me.

I WASN'T
SCARED
OR ANYTHING . . .

I was just really pleased . . . that's all!

I quickly whispered what was going on to everyone and we all went in together. Even Walter came along!

We sneaked down the hall towards our classroom. Luckily, Angel Face had brought a torch so we could see where we were going.

When we got to our classroom door, we could hear noises coming from inside, so we sneaked up and pushed it open quietly.

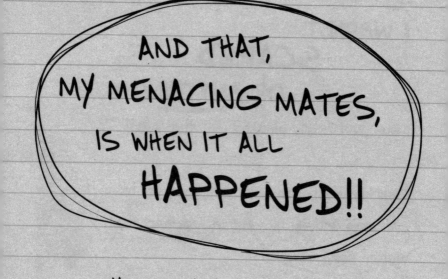

AND THAT,
MY MENACING MATES,
IS WHEN IT ALL
HAPPENED!!

Minnie reached inside the door and flicked the light on and . . .

It was Creech! She had her back to us and was writing BUM-FACE on the chalkboard . . .

Mrs Creecher!?!?

Walter suddenly
plucked up a gust
of courage from
somewhere and
stepped into the
room . . .

MRS CREECHER!
I AM APPALLED!

But Creecher just kept on doodling on the
board. Maybe she hadn't heard us?

Next Minnie had
a go . . .

CREECHER!
HEY!?!

Mrs Creecher still didn't seem to hear us, so I thought I'd try shouting . . . Y'know . . . just to see . . .

OY! BUM-FACE!

Mrs Creecher slowly turned round and shuffled towards her desk. Before we could stop her, she grabbed it by the edge and flipped it over . . . **We all gasped**, but it was then that we noticed her eyes were closed. Creecher tilted her head back and let rip a **big, fat** snoring sound.

SHE WAS ASLEEP!

The crusty old grunion was **sleep-MENACING!**

So that was the mystery over, my merry
band of Menaces.

Old Creecher had been so shocked by
reading my diaries that she started acting
out in her sleep all the **BRILLIANT**
menacing lessons she'd learned.

Sergeant Slipper eventually arrived at Bash
Street School and woke the Booky Bum-
Face up. He took her down to Beanotown
Police Station, but they eventually let her go
because apparently you can't be blamed for
something you do in your sleep . . .

Which gives me the
<u>**BEST**</u> idea ever!

CAN'T GET INTO TROUBLE FOR
ANYTHING YOU DO IN YOUR SLEEP????

I'VE GOT THE REST OF THE SCHOOL
HOLIDAYS AND LOADS OF MENACING
TO BE GETTING ON WITH . . . ONLY
THIS TIME . . . I'M DOING IT WITH MY
EYES CLOSED!! HA!

WANT MORE DENNIS?

LISTEN TO THE AUDIOBOOK AND HEAR ALL THE MADNESS AND MAYHEM (AND LOUD BURPS . . . EWWWW!) AS THE AMAZING STEVEN BUTLER BRINGS DENNIS TO LIFE.

GO TO THE PUFFIN PODCAST SOUNDCLOUD PAGE AND FIND THE DENNIS THE MENACE PLAYLIST TO LISTEN TO A FREE CHAPTER!

DO IT NOW!

AVAILABLE AS AUDIOBOOKS

Scan the QR code to listen to an extract

http://snd.sc/1luGmbA

THE BEANO
Where's Dennis?

NEW 'WHERE'S DENNIS?'* APP!
OUT NOW! FREE TO DOWNLOAD!

Over 50 things to find in each scene, plus a two-player head-to-head mode, beat the clock and more.

What are you waiting for? Go download it and get searching! Ask your parents first, of course, or they'll go bonkers.

Download on the App Store

ANDROID APP ON Google play

Got no tablety thingy? No worries. Just get the good ol' fashioned book instead!

Available in all good bookshops (and maybe even some rubbish ones!)

*AND GNASHER!

WHY NOT DO YOUR OWN MENACE JOURNAL?

I've menaced my diary . . . now it's time to menace yours!

Join *The Beano* comic's front-page legend as he guides you through everything you need to know to create a book just like his. Your teacher will hate it!

STICKY MAYHEM WITH THE BEANO GANG!

Packed to the rafters with puzzles, activities, funnies and over one thousand stickers of all your Beano favourites, from Dennis and Gnasher to Calamity James and the Bash Street Kids.

KIDS RULE IN BEANOTOWN!

WANT MORE DENNIS THE MENACE?
JOIN HIM EVERY WEDNESDAY IN . . .

THE BEANO®

www.beano.com

© DC THOMSON & CO. LTD. 2014